CHALK

CHALK

by

DOUG DIACZUK

WINNER OF THE

38TH ANNUAL

3-DAY NOVEL WRITING

CONTEST

ANVIL PRESS / VANCOUVER

Copyright © 2016 by Doug Diaczuk

All rights reserved. No part of this book may be reproduced by any means without the prior written permission of the publisher, with the exception of brief passages in reviews. Any request for photocopying or other reprographic copying of any part of this book must be directed in writing to access: The Canadian Copyright Licensing Agency, One Yonge Street, Suite 800, Toronto, Ontario, Canada, M5E 1E5.

Anvil Press Publishers Inc.
P.O. Box 3008, Main Post Office
Vancouver, B.C. V6B 3X5 CANADA
www.anvilpress.com

Library and Archives Canada Cataloguing in Publication

Diaczuk, Doug, author
    Chalk / Doug Diaczuk. — 1st edition.

Winner of the 38th Annual 3-Day Novel Contest.
ISBN 978-1-77214-078-1 (paperback)

    I. Title.

PS8607.I213C43 2016   C813'.6   C2016-903991-9

Printed and bound in Canada
Cover design by Derek von Essen
Interior by HeimatHouse
Represented in Canada by the Publishers Group Canada
Distributed by Raincoast Books

The publisher gratefully acknowledges the financial assistance of the Canada Council for the Arts, the Canada Book Fund, and the Province of British Columbia through the B.C. Arts Council and the Book Publishing Tax Credit.

For J. M. W.

"There's always something within us that wants to be noticed, to be held within someone's gaze, for how else might we be loved? Even in our lowest moments, when our desire for invisibility is at its greatest, there will always be that little voice that softly cries out, against all hope and reason, look at me, see me."

—Jonathan Goldstein, "Being Invisible,"
Wiretap – CBC Radio One

I

Chalk Flowers

This is you. You are thirty years old, single, and live in a one-bedroom apartment with beige-coloured walls, a television with a snowy screen, and curtains that diffuse light rather than block it. You lie awake in the sickeningly yellow morning light, staring up at the ceiling, trying to think of a reason to get out of bed. This is your life.

You walk into the grocery store and sing the song playing on the intercom quietly under your breath. The same songs play on an endless loop on a Tuesday afternoon and you feel sorry for the employees who have to listen to the same songs over and over again for eight hours a day. In the frozen food aisle, a tall, skinny kid offers you a sample of cheese on a toothpick. You take one and comment that it is sharp because you remember seeing the word sharp on a block of cheddar cheese once. You ask for another one. You say again that it is sharp, sharper than the last sample and you take another without asking. The kid does not stop you, so you take another, and then another, until your mouth is full of sharp cheese and your hand cradles a miniature woodpile of used toothpicks. Through your stuffed mouth you ask why the cheese samples are being handed out in the frozen foods section and the kid looks through you at the frozen pizzas in the case behind you and doesn't say anything. You place the toothpicks on the blue tablecloth because there is no garbage can and you thank him for the cheese and tell him that you might buy some. When you get to the aisle with the blocks of cheese stacked like bricks, you look for the word sharp, but can't find it anywhere, so you move along, a little dismayed and ashamed for having lied.

At the express checkout, a young woman with her hair tied in a ponytail slightly off-centre starts to ring through your items. About halfway through your order she stops and you can see by the way her eyes dart back and forth, and the nearly imperceptible way her lips move, that she is counting how many items you have. It's over twelve. I'm sorry, she says, the minty freshness of her gum reaching you on the other side of the black conveyor belt that holds your thirteen items, you have too many items. You will have to put something back. Can you make an exception? you ask. Sorry, rules are rules. You pick up a jar of green olives and hand them to her, saying that you don't really care for olives anyway. She stands there, holding the jar, unsure of what to do with it, then she places it on the edge of the till, next to the register and the "this till is closed" sign, and you ask what will happen to the jar now. She ignores your question and brushes the items over the red blinking light under a piece of glass until it beeps and then she moves on to the next. You tell her she's ugly. She ignores you, and when she finishes scanning the items, she punches in a total and announces it to you with little enthusiasm. She looks directly through you to the shelf of candy bars and celebrity magazines. You've said this to her before and she thinks that you say it because you are just as ugly on the inside. It doesn't change that she is ugly on the outside. You turn around, as though you are trying to figure out what she is looking at, and pick up a magazine with a photo of a woman with large fake lips and large fake breasts and place it on the conveyor belt and say, this too.

ON THE BUS there are no seats, so you sit down on the lap of a very large man whose body spills out onto a second seat. You can feel his breath on the back of your neck. It is hot and moist and smells of onions or sharp cheddar cheese. He tries to move you by bucking his stomach and you're tempted to say wee, but instead you brace yourself against the seat in front of you, your grocery bags knocking back and forth, the cans of tomato soup colliding with the jar of peanut butter and the carton of milk just sitting there. What's the matter with you? Get off me, the fat man says. You give him a half turn and say, oh, I'm sorry, is this seat taken? He pushes you off and you nearly fall over but catch yourself in time. Raising one of your plastic bags, you point to the half seat next to him and ask if that one is taken, too. He looks past you and out the window at the passing cars and colourful graffiti on the colourless walls of the buildings. The other passengers grip the bags resting on their laps a little tighter as you scan the rest of the bus looking for a seat. You can't hold onto anything because the white plastic handles of the grocery bags are wrapped around your hands, turning your fingers bright red. You stand in the middle of the aisle, feet apart, leaning backward and forward with the motion of the bus, using your grocery bags for balance.

On the walk from the bus stop to your building you take care to step around every piece of garbage. You live in perpetual fear that you will bring home something on your shoe that you never intended to—a cigarette butt, a piece of gum, a used condom, a flyer advertising discount laser eye surgery. On the sidewalk outside of your building, two little girls are drawing flowers in brightly coloured chalk and you have to step around them. You pause and look down at the drawings, admiring their dedication to the craft. What is it? you ask. The little girl closest to you says, with the matter-of-factness of a child, that it is a flower. What kind of flower? She looks down at the sidewalk and thinks for a moment. Her hands are covered in blue and pink dust and you try to imagine what the city would look like if all the dirt was as colourful as the little girl's hands. You grow tired of waiting for an answer and say that it doesn't look like any flower that you have ever seen before. Both girls look up at you with blank faces and then continue to shade in the petals of this strange, alien flower, each one a different colour.

Outside your building, a man with thinning brown hair combed over a shining bald head waves to you and says hello. You cannot wave back because your arms are weighted down from carrying your grocery bags and you don't say hello back because you don't know who this man is. When he gets closer he apologizes and says that he thought you were someone else. Who did you think I was? you ask. He tells you that it's not important and apologizes and then walks on. As you walk up the steps to your building you watch the man casually walking down the sidewalk, the back of his head balding even more than the top, and you wonder who he thought you were and why you can't be that person. Before entering the building, you lift up your feet one at a time and examine the bottoms of your shoes.

Later that night you invite a friend over that you don't particularly like. You drink a beer in your bedroom before he comes and hide the empty can under your bed with the dozen or so full ones. You drink another one, knowing that he will be late. When he arrives, you offer him a beer and tell him that there are some in the fridge. He tells you that there are none and you say that you must have forgotten to pick some up. You offer him green olives instead but he says that he doesn't like olives. You spend the evening playing Nintendo. When you beat him you rub it in his face and tell him that he is a loser. What you don't tell him is that you've been practicing all week just so you could beat him and call him a loser.

He asks if you want to go get a drink at a bar but you tell him that you're pretty tired, so he leaves on his own in search of alcohol and a woman with large breasts and red hair that he spent an uncomfortable amount of time describing to you earlier that evening. After you retrieve the beer from under your bed and put it back in the fridge, you drink several more and watch video clips online. You find a clip of a politician shooting himself on live TV and you wonder why you've never heard of this before. The video is fuzzy and it is difficult to make anything out, but the existence of this clip unsettles you. For the rest of the night you wonder if the blood from the back of your head would create pretty floral patterns on the wall behind the couch and whether or not the building manager or police officer or fireman or neighbour would comment on how pretty the patterns look when they find you a week from now.

At work you place a paper clamp on the end of your finger and leave it there until your finger turns dark purple. You start to worry that your tie is too tight and that your face will turn the same colour and will frighten your co-workers. You turn to the woman in the opposite cubicle and tell her that in 1991 a politician shot himself on live TV and that there is a video of it just because you decide that people should be warned that something like that exists out there and they should prepare themselves for it just in case they happen to stumble upon it late in the night.

In a meeting you sit opposite the large windows so you can look out at the tops of the other buildings. What would happen if there was a fire and we were trapped in here, you wonder. You like to think that you would jump out the window with everyone else, but you're not so sure. Then you wonder how it would feel if you were ever sucked out of an airplane flying at thirty thousand feet in the air still strapped to your seat. If you are wearing enough clothes, you can hold them out and slow down your descent like cartoon characters do and if you are above water, you can point your feet down and slip beneath the surface like a pencil, push off from the bottom, and resurface unhurt. But then you remember reading that the velocity is so great that your clothes will be torn from your body as you fall and you will become nothing but a naked body flying through the air, unable to breathe because the air is too thin to enter your lungs, and that hitting water at that speed is just like hitting concrete. Afterwards your supervisor asks if you have a firm grasp on the strategy laid out during the meeting. You tell him that it hit you like a body hitting concrete.

That evening you decide to go to a movie just because you don't know what else to do. You clap after every preview because you once saw an old man do this in a theatre when you were a kid and it made you sad. You fall asleep halfway through the movie, which surprises you because when it first started you were annoyed by how loud the sound was. You leave just before the movie ends, nearly running down the stairs with the thin strip of lights. You only trip once and walk back out into the bright lights of the lobby and you wonder why the old man in the theatre used to clap for the previews and left before the movie ended.

When you wake up the next morning you lay in bed for a long time, pulling at the skin on the top of your hand to see if you are dehydrated. The phone rings and you let it ring until the machine picks up. Your mother leaves a long message about how Marie had her baby and that mother and baby are doing just fine and that the baby looks like Marie. You think about your own children, the ones you will never meet, and you wonder what you would say to them now if given the chance. You get up and look for an old issue of *National Geographic*. When you find it, you flip to the article about overpopulation and how the world's population will reach nine billion by the year 2040 and you think that Marie is part of the problem.

Two days later you run into your girlfriend in a park. It has been seventy-six days since you last saw her. She smiles when she sees you and is acting unusually friendly. You talk about work and she asks you how therapy is going. You lie and tell her that it is really helping, though going to therapy was only something you told her you would do to make her think that you were capable of becoming a better person. You are in the midst of complimenting her shoes when she tells you, rather abruptly, that she is engaged. You congratulate her with every last bit of sincerity you can scrape off the soles of your feet and she tells you not to worry, that you will find someone. You laugh on the inside before dying a little and agree out loud that there is someone out there for everyone. You clench your fists inside your pockets and try to keep your entire body from shaking. You know what's coming next, so you congratulate her again and then start walking in the opposite direction.

You cry loudly on the bus ride home making the other passengers uncomfortable. You renew your vows never to fall in love again and this makes you feel a little better but the other passengers even worse. You tell a woman sitting across from you that she is beautiful and she smiles awkwardly, looking to the other passengers for some kind of assistance. You ask her out on a date and her cheeks turn red and she tells you that she is seeing someone. You congratulate her and get off at the next stop.

You decide that you deserve a reward for handling the encounter in the park so well and you go to the zoo. You throw empty peanut shells into the open enclosures until you are told to stop by a zoo employee. You spend the next half hour standing in front of a glass cage, looking through the invisible bars, the illusion of freedom, or maybe imprisonment, and watch a gorilla that appears to be licking its fingers, but the leathery grey skin never changes colour and its eyes never look away from the sky.

That evening you drink the rest of the beer in the fridge, putting on a single shoe to crush the cans when they are empty. The TV is on but you are not watching it. The week's events play over and over again in your head—falling out of the office window, landing in the ocean but never touching the bottom, your girlfriend looking so beautiful, the girl on the bus looking so afraid, and the gorilla lapping its strange tongue across its fingers over and over again. Your head starts to bob up and down and you feel like you could sleep for days so you pour out the last half of the last beer and leave the empty can on the kitchen counter. You fall asleep on the couch with the TV tuned to the weather channel and still wearing one shoe.

The next day you are too hungover to go to work so you call in sick. You spend most of the morning debating whether you should go in ever again and you decide that you will see how you feel tomorrow morning. You watch a pornographic movie but you are still too hungover to masturbate, so with unusual clarity you wonder what the actress's breasts feel like in real life. She says that her breasts are so soft to the camera and you thank her for her honesty. After you finish masturbating, you no longer wonder what her breasts feel like or if they really are as soft as she says.

At work you stick the end of a staple into your index finger and squeeze out a drop of blood. You touch the finger to your front teeth and taste the richness of the blood, though you wonder if you are actually tasting the dirty metal of the staple. You start to worry that there are bloodstains on your teeth, which could upset your co-workers, so you walk to the bathroom without talking to anyone and examine your teeth in the mirror. You cannot see any blood on your teeth even though you can still taste it.

There is a message on the answering machine from your mother when you get home. You can hear the worry in her voice as she strains to tell you that Marie's baby is still in the hospital. You play the message again and listen to the sound of your mother's voice. It sounds so small, like it could fit inside the little black machine, smaller still to fit on a single side of the tape in the cassette. *Things are looking bad, you really should come, Marie needs the support.* You stand in the hallway in front of the machine still holding onto your briefcase and running your tongue over your teeth. You secretly feel guilty for wishing something bad would happen to someone, even though you never specifically wished anything bad would happen to Marie or her baby.

You call your girlfriend and tell her about Marie's baby. She shows genuine concern and then you tell her that you can still taste blood on your teeth and she tells you that she has to go. You practice playing video games for two hours and then call your friend and ask him if he would like to come over and to bring something to drink. He tells you that he can't tonight because he has a date. You tell him that you hate him and that he can never come over again because he is a loser. He laughs at this and you hang up the phone, fairly certain that you will never talk to him again.

You place two six-packs and a tin of mints on the conveyor belt and ask the ugly cashier if this counts as thirteen items. She rings your order through without saying anything and when she hands you your receipt you lie and tell her that she is beautiful. She looks right through you to the large storefront windows where the bus you were supposed to catch speeds by. Rather than wait for the next one, you decide to walk the fourteen blocks back to your building. At the fourth bus stop down the street you see the fat man sitting on the bench. You sit down next to him and ask him how his day is going. He doesn't remember you and he tells you that this day is just like any other day and you laugh louder than is necessary. He shakes his head and rests his arms on his belly that nearly extends past his knees and he makes you feel small. You tell him that he is beautiful, too, and he tells you to go fuck yourself. I think I'll walk the rest of the way home, you say, and stand up, extending a hand to bid the man farewell. He looks at it and then looks past you for the bus that is two stops down. It was nice talking with you, you say, then pick up your bags and start back down the street.

You step over the flower that you have never seen before and walk around it in circles to try and look at it from different perspectives. Colourful footprints extend in both directions down the sidewalk from the countless feet that have stepped on this strange colourful flower. The little girls are not there. All that is left of them is a tiny piece of chalk in the middle of the flower. You pick it up and it crumbles in your hands, leaving your palms covered in a thin layer of blue dust.

Upstairs, the red light on your answering machine is flashing and you stand in front of the machine, motionless, with the bags wrapped around your hands. You stay there for almost ten minutes, then you walk away and put the beer in the bathtub and pop a mint into your mouth. The taste of blood disappears and you sit on the couch and watch the red light on the answering machine blink. You turn on the TV and watch a show about alligators in a swamp. Some of the smaller alligators run on the sand and move at surprising speeds and it is unsettling.

The phone rings and your eyes dart away from a pair of eyes poking out above the green water. The phone keeps ringing until finally the machine picks up. The red light stops flashing and there is a pause and then a click and then the little red light starts flashing again. You turn off the TV and hear the rain. At the window you look down at the sidewalk and watch as the flower that you didn't recognize slowly washes away, a river of blue and pink and purple flowing into the gutter, and you realize that you will never see that particular flower ever again.

II

Chalk Memories

You take up smoking again just because you want something to look forward to when you wake up in the morning. You stand on the sidewalk in front of your building under the purple morning sky, your head spinning from the small high you get from inhaling the tobacco. You feel like you might be sick, but you convince yourself that things will get better and keep smoking. There are no cars on the street, the sidewalk is empty, and everything is quiet. You might just stay here and watch the sunrise, but the time it takes you to smoke a single cigarette isn't long enough, so you go back inside and lay on the couch, and wait for the room to stop spinning.

There is nothing on TV this early in the morning, but you somehow become drawn into late-night infomercials advertising quick ways to lose weight or increase your sexual prowess and you laugh at how difficult everything seems to be in the world. If only life were really that difficult. You change the channel to the twenty-four-hour news network hoping to come across a breaking story and become the first person in the city to learn of some great tragedy, but the news anchor just rattles off numbers of a corporate merger that you couldn't care less about.

You look away from the TV and stare at the ceiling, hoping for sleep that doesn't come, while debating whether or not you could get away with smoking a cigarette next to an open window without setting off the fire alarm. Red lights begin flashing on the wall as though the thought alone was enough to cause someone to call 9-1-1. You leave your apartment and pass two firemen in the stairwell: one carrying an axe, the other a large bag with a white cross on it. Outside, you light a cigarette and watch two other firemen enter the building. The red lights continue to spin from the truck and an ambulance pulls up behind it. You stumble on the sidewalk, feeling dizzy from your second cigarette since quitting almost two years ago, and you immediately light another one. Is the building on fire? you ask one of the firefighters standing nearest the truck. He doesn't answer you, so you look skyward, expecting to see flames shooting out from a fourth floor window and bodies hurtling down to the sidewalk.

I really admire what you do, you tell the fireman. It must be exciting to be one of the few people to really see the city asleep. The fireman tucks his chin into his shoulder and talks into his radio. Two firemen exit the building and take off their helmets. Do you get a lot of false alarms? you ask. The fireman tells you to stand back so you take three steps back. Turn off those damn lights, he says, and the street goes dark again. You flick your cigarette on the sidewalk in the path of another exiting fireman and tell him that he missed a spot.

When you try to re-enter the building, you are told again to stand clear. But I live here, you try to explain, but the fireman with the radio attached to his shoulder pushes you back from the steps and tells you to wait a moment. You ask if you can sit on the front of his truck, just like you did when you were in high school and a student sprayed pepper spray in the hall and the entire school was evacuated and a fireman invited you and your friends to sit on the front of the truck because it was warm. He doesn't answer so you sit on the shiny chrome bumper and spin an unlit cigarette between your fingers.

By the time you toss away your fourth cigarette since quitting two years ago, the door to the building opens and the paramedics bring down your neighbour on a gurney. Her body is covered in a white sheet and her eyes are closed. Is she dead? you ask when she is wheeled past. Step back, please.

The ambulance drives away and the other firefighters load the equipment back into the truck and tell you that you can return to your apartment. The sun is rising down the street and you are tempted to mark the occasion with another cigarette, but if you do, you are certain that you will throw up. You thank the firefighters and they smile and nod. You watch as the truck pulls away from the curb, the lights silent, and the sun casting the buildings in a purple hue. The start of a new day.

You learn the next day that your neighbour, a sixty-seven-year-old woman who lived alone, has died. A police officer stands in her doorway and you watch him from your peephole. He props open the door with a garbage can and steps inside. Seeing your opportunity, you gather old issues of *TV Guide* and a couple soup cans into a garbage bag and step into the hall. You enter your neighbour's apartment and stand in the doorway. You rarely saw her and her existence meant little to you, but now, standing in the doorway to her apartment, you want to know where she died, where she was found, the place in this apartment where she took her last breath. It's such an intimate detail—knowing where someone died. But you decide that because you saw her leave the building, already dead, you feel entitled to know this information. So you go on, stepping further into the apartment of a woman that you lived across from for over a year but never really knew. Just as you are about to enter the living room, the police officer from the doorway steps out from the kitchenette and places a hand on your chest. What are you doing here? he asks. I'm just . . . You need to leave, he tells you. You hold up your bag of garbage and tell him that you knew the sixty-seven-year-old woman.

Were you close? he asks.

Yes, you lie.

I'm sorry, but you need to leave.

You try to look over his shoulder, to the living room where you imagine she was found. You want to see the chalk lines of her body on the living room floor.

Is that where it happened? you ask, pointing over the officer's shoulder.

Where what happened?

Where she died. Is it there?

Come with me, the officer says, pushing you back. You jump up and catch a glimpse of the living room floor. The only thing you see is a small, dark stain on the carpet. Do you still use chalk, or is it tape now? you ask. The officer takes the bag of garbage from you and places it at your feet.

YOU STICK YOUR HANDS out between the bars of the jail cell just because you've seen people do this in movies. It feels natural. The first question you are asked is if you have done any drugs or have been drinking.

Does smoking count as a drug?

No.

Then no.

Why were you in her apartment?

I was curious.

Curious of what?

Of what happened.

What happened?

I don't know.

She may have been killed.

I already know that.

You don't understand, she may have been murdered.

So then there's an investigation?

Yes, it is ongoing.

Do you still use chalk?

It's uncomfortably bright in your cell and you run your hands over the freshly painted white walls and think that this isn't so bad. Somewhere down the corridor you hear the drunks picked up the night before wake up and cry out for help. What a feeling, you think, and secretly wish that you were waking up with them, still drunk, or just drunk enough to not care what was happening, but sober enough to know that it isn't right.

It is determined that your neighbour died of natural causes, natural being a brain aneurysm that rendered her body dead before it hit the floor in the living room, her head passing by the edge of the coffee table on the way down. Her son called the police when she didn't answer her phone, but you don't remember her even having a son. She was lying dead in her apartment for at least a day. Who was forgotten by whom? you wonder. It's not wise to wander into apartments of the recently deceased, you are told by an officer when released, and you tell him that it is the best advice you have ever received.

WHEN YOU LEAVE for work the next morning, you pause in front of the door to the apartment that is now empty. People die every day and people die across from other apartments, too. Last night it happened to be your apartment. What do those people do? How do they go on? You turn away from the door to the apartment of a woman you rarely saw and walk to the stairwell. It's that simple.

At work you announce that your neighbour passed away, just because you like to watch how your co-workers react to the news. I'm so sorry to hear that, is the most common response, and then they go about their work as though proper formality somehow sustains life. It's really tough, you say, she was like a mother to me. The middle-aged, single mother from human resources hugs you and says that you are welcome to take the rest of the day off if you'd like. She smells of vanilla and you decide to stop for ice cream on your way back to the apartment. You spend the rest of the afternoon lying on your living room floor, trying to understand what an aneurysm is, how it happens, and whether or not it is about to happen in your brain the entire time that you remain on the floor.

IN THE WAITING room of the doctor's office you read an article in *Maclean's Magazine* about new revelations regarding bodies exhumed in the Arctic from Franklin's lost expedition. There are several photographs of men who have been dead for over 120 years and the expressions on the faces look surprised to see a living person after all that time in the dark. It's strange reading material for a doctor's office and you stare into their dead eyes, eyes that are still open, eyes that are still there, and you wonder what they see. You wish that you could die in the Arctic, for no other reason than to be exhumed hundreds of years after your death, and once again look out at the world and allow the living to see your eyes.

What causes an aneurysm? you ask your doctor.

That's not something you need to worry about.

But if it was something I needed to worry about, how might I prevent it? He writes something on your chart and then turns to you and tells you to lie down on the paper-covered table. Are you smoking again? he asks, noticing the stains on your fingers. Yes, you admit. He makes a note on your chart. It's a tough habit to break, he tells you, adding that he knows first-hand, he himself being a smoker for almost forty years. As you put your clothes back on, you tell your doctor that you will be getting on a plane next week and that you are afraid you will die. He chuckles and tells you that there is no reason to be afraid.

It's just, if something goes wrong, if the plane starts to go down, I don't want to be aware of it.

Many people are afraid of flying. Just remember, you are more likely to die on your way to the airport than in an air disaster.

This doesn't help you and you ask if there is anything he can prescribe to ease the stress of getting on the plane.

Is it that bad?

I'm convinced that I'm going to die if I get on that plane.

The pharmacist doesn't offer any more useful information than your doctor on the likelihood of dying from an aneurysm. He *does* tell you that you need to take the pills your doctor prescribed on a full stomach, as they are likely to cause stomach upset. On the bus, you shake the bottle of pills near your ear and take off the cap to smell them, then place the bottle back in the small paper bag. You turn to a young kid with large headphones over his faded, black toque and tell him that these should fucking knock you right out. What? he says, lowering his headphones. Louder, you tell him that these pills should knock you the fuck out and that now you won't die on the airplane. He puts the headphones back in place, but you shuffle closer and keep talking.

Because if you aren't aware that you're about to crash into the ground at five hundred miles per hour, it doesn't really matter, does it? He nods, but you are not convinced that he has heard you. Does it?

What? he says, pulling the headphones back down again.

If you're already dead inside, a plane crash is meaningless, right?

Planes don't crash very often, he tells you.

Some do.

You're more likely to be killed on the way to the airport.

You pop two pills into your mouth and hold the open bottle toward him. If we crash right now, it won't matter, because we'll already be dead on the inside.

THERE ARE EXACTLY twenty-four hours until you have to board the plane. You wake up next to your open suitcase and, at first, you are convinced that the pills you were prescribed knocked you out for a week and that you just arrived back home. You don't remember getting off the bus or getting home, but you see that the bottle of pills on your night stand is still full. Examining the bottle, you realize that you forgot to ask if the side effects include an increased risk of brain aneurysms. You hope that there is an increased risk, maybe even the possibility of willing it to happen in your brain with enough concentration, so when the plane starts to break up in the air, you can focus on a specific part in your brain and cause it to explode in the greatest aneurysm ever known to man. You take two more pills and lie back down with one foot in your empty suitcase. You have more than enough to get you there and back, so two more won't hurt. Before you fall back asleep, you think about your brain, the front, just behind your eyes, but not too hard. You want to save any explosions for when you are in the air.

With your suitcase packed, you stand in front of the answering machine. The little red light is still blinking. You call your mother to tell her that you are on your way home, but the phone keeps ringing, so you hang up. You pick up the phone again and call your girlfriend to tell her that you will be going away for a week and that you love her just in case something goes wrong thirty thousand feet in the air. There is no answer, so you leave her a message, telling her that you have to go back home and that things are looking bad for Marie. You pause and then tell her that you will wave to her from above when the plane passes over the city.

AIRPORTS ARE DEPRESSING, just like all the other transitional places where people are always coming and going. It's like a hospital. It bothers you how calm everyone is as they walk down the endlessly long corridors with window-lined walls, pulling suitcases with one hand and stuffing cold bagels into their mouths with the other. Children scream as they are dragged around by fretful parents, some stopping to look out the large windows at the parked planes. For the businessmen, who wear fine suits when travelling so they don't have to pack them, it's all routine, as though the possibility of dying by getting sucked out of a plane is an acceptable job hazard.

It's strange to see the outside of the plane visible in the space between the gangway and the open door. You touch it, because you know that soon it will be exposed to the frigid air of high altitudes. You knock on it with your knuckle and are told not to do that by the flight attendant waiting to take your boarding pass. The width of her smile is unsettling, revealing a set of large teeth that can, in fact, against all reason, be covered by her thick, dark painted lips. You take your window seat in the middle of the plane overlooking the left wing. You are soon joined by a man wearing a grey suit and a lavender tie. You introduce yourself and hold out your hand. He pulls out a copy of *The Economist* and tells you that he makes a point of not touching people on airplanes. That's a good policy, you say, your hand still hovering over his armrest.

Do you know how long the flight is? I forgot to double check.

Where are you going?

Home.

You can put your hand down, he says, and you sit back in your seat. It's about three and a half hours, give or take.

Give or take what? you ask. He doesn't answer. You thank the man and then turn to him again and ask if the suit he is wearing is the only suit he owns. He clears his throat and turns back to *The Economist*.

At the first movement of the plane, backward, pulling away from the terminal, you realize that you forgot to take any pills. You pop the cap and tap out four pills. You take two and hold out your hand to the man next to you. He ignores the offer, so you put them back in the bottle. You press the call button for the stewardess and she arrives with her large grin and you ask for a glass of water.

I'm sorry, we are about to take off. Drink service will begin shortly after.

But I need to take my medication.

Can it wait? The pills in your mouth rattle against your teeth, toyed with by your tongue, and you nod.

You try to make idle conversation with the man next to you as you are pushed back in your seat when the plane takes off. He ignores you, still reading an article on trade agreements in East Asia, as if the sensation of speeding down a runway and then lifting off the ground means nothing to him. Flying is so surreal and it is difficult to wrap your mind around the fact that you are sitting in a tube flying five hundred miles per hour, climbing to thirty thousand feet above the ground. Even looking out the window, seeing the ground below, doesn't seem real. By the time the flight attendant comes around with drinks, the pills in your mouth are nearly dissolved under your tongue. You take out two more and ask the man next to you if he wants any.

They are meant to calm you when flying, you explain.

You shouldn't drug yourself when flying, he says, because you won't be able to react properly in an emergency.

You swallow the tiny pieces of pill that remain in your mouth and drop the other two back into the bottle.

You press your forehead to the plastic glass of the window. The wing seems to bend with the movement of the plane so you look past it to the ground. Green fields intersected by roads and highways glide past below. You see houses, little white buildings that look so isolated from above. You imagine a little girl is standing on the porch of one of these houses, looking up at the clear blue sky, watching the vapour trails of your plane as it flies overhead. You wonder whether or not there is a faint thought in the back of her head that the plane that she is watching might fall from the sky and she will witness the deaths of 282 people from her front porch. You ring for the flight attendant and you compliment her smile. Leaning over the man beside you, you ask if she is ever afraid.

Afraid of what?

You know, crashing.

The man beside you grunts and the stewardess smiles to comfort you, adding that there is nothing to be afraid of, that planes are perfectly safe.

But do you ever get a little nervous, thinking that maybe something might go wrong?

Sweetie, this is my fourth flight today. I have been doing this for seven years and never once has that thought ever entered my mind. Just sit back and relax. You are perfectly safe.

You sit back in your seat and the man next to you has rolled up his magazine and taps it against his knee. You can tell that he wants to hit you with it.

There is a bump in the sky, as though the plane has just flown over a floating rock. Then another and another. The seatbelt light starts to flash and the captain comes over the intercom informing the passengers that the flight will be experiencing some slight turbulence. There is another bump, and then the plane dips. The man next to you rests his head against the back of the seat and closes his eyes. You unbuckle your seat belt and stand, looking at all the closed eyes around you. The flight attendant tells you to please take your seat and buckle your seat belt. There is another bump, more violent this time, and you fall over the lap of the man next to you. He tries to push you off and then the lights in the cabin flicker. Someone from the back of the plane screams. You look to the front, at the flight attendant buckled into her small folding chair near the entrance. Her eyes are closed, too, and her giant teeth bite down into her bottom lip and you can see that she is afraid. The man next to you is able to push you back into your seat. You buckle up your seat belt, fight to get two more pills from the little orange bottle and into your bloodstream, press your face to the plastic glass of the window, and watch the wing move up and down with the turbulence, ready to break free. You look past it, down at the little houses in the fields, to the little girls on front porches who look up at the clear blue sky, and are about to witness the deaths of 282 people.

YOU TRY TO stand but are held in place by your seat belt. The man who was sitting next to you is standing and pulling his bag out of the overhead compartment. You offer to sell him your return ticket, but he turns away and follows the other passengers down the aisle. Once you are freed from your seat belt, you try to stand, but you feel like you might pass out. You've been in the sky for too long and can't adjust to the pull of the earth in which you are not so close. The flight attendant, who is collecting empty cups and pop cans, tells you that you need to deplane. You're the only one left and you stand by bracing yourself on the seats. Standing close enough to the flight attendant to see the lipstick stains on her teeth, you offer to buy her a drink to ease the edge of almost dying. She politely declines your offer and she tells you that it's natural to be afraid, adding that the little rough spot the plane hit was really nothing at all. You tell her that she's crazy and that she should consider a career change. She smiles at you one last time when you step off the plane and head down the empty gangway.

Your suitcase is the only one left spinning around the carousel. You watch it go past twice, the piece of red yarn tied to the handle disappearing under the rubber flaps at the end, and then reappearing on the other side. Outside, you light a cigarette and smoke half of it before throwing up in a garbage can next to the bus stop. On the bus, you lie down in the middle of the aisle in front of your suitcase and the driver yells at you twice to stand, but you ignore him. The rocking of the bus back and forth on its air suspension makes you feel like you are still flying and all you can see from this vantage point are the ankles of the other passengers and the sky through the windows. An older gentleman hoists you up by your arms and gently taps your cheek.

You all right, son?

I think I'm having an aneurysm, you say.

He lets you go, either from shock or disgust, and you fall back down. No one helps you up again and passengers step over your prone body to get off at the next stop, and the new passengers that get on don't seem to notice that you are even there.

You pull yourself along the aisle of the bus by grabbing onto the legs of the seats and the people sitting on them. You reach the front and ask the driver how much longer it is until your stop. He doesn't answer, so you repeat the question loud enough for everyone on the bus to hear you, but still, no one provides an answer. The bus comes to a stop and the driver grabs you under the arms and pulls you to your feet. Then he stuffs a pink ticket in your front pocket and carries you off the bus, sitting you down on a bench in a little glass box. You need to transfer to the crosstown route, he tells you, then gets back on the bus and seals the doors. You try to follow, but bump your shoulder into the glass wall and spin around and fall to the sidewalk. The bus roars away, its back engine sounding as loud as a jet, and you realize that your suitcase with the red piece of yarn tied to the handle is still in the middle of the aisle. You look down at the dark smudges on the front of your shirt from all the feet walking across the dirty bus floor and wish that you had put on your best suit that morning before heading to the airport.

IN THE AISLES of a department store, your aneurysm goes away and the ground starts to feel normal again. The pills mostly wore off during your nap on the sidewalk at the bus stop, and though you still feel tired enough to lie down under a rack of shirts and fall asleep, you have adjusted to the pull of the earth and you no longer feel dizzy or light-headed. You walk past the racks of clothes for boys and girls, soaking in the nostalgia from the pictures of Spider-man and Batman in heroic poses on pairs of black jogging pants. You decide on a lavender-coloured shirt and you are a little disappointed that there are no superheroes on button-downed lavender shirts. You change into your new clothes and look for a gift for Marie's baby. You decide on a pail of sidewalk chalk because of the little girls you saw drawing those strange flowers in front of your building. You hold up the cuff of the shirt to the cashier so she can scan the tag, and you sit on the conveyor belt so she can get the one on the back of your pants. We don't normally allow people to wear their purchases out of the store, the cashier tells you. You ask for a knife to cut the tags off, but she tells you that she doesn't have one, so you ask for scissors. She looks under the till and you notice a tattoo of a butterfly on the back of her neck. It's faded and stretched from weight gain after the fact. It's then that you remember her and immediately regret handing her your credit card.

Oh my God, I thought you looked familiar. How have you been?

I've been fine, thank you.

I thought you left town years ago.

I'm here visiting Marie.

Oh, right. I heard. The poor thing. You sign your bill and ask for a bag for your dirty clothes.

How long are you in town for? We should get together and catch up.

Catch up on what?

You know, everything. She hands you a piece of paper with her phone number on it and a smiley face at the bottom. You try to remember when she got the tattoo, how it looked when she was young, and her name.

YOU STAND ON the sidewalk outside your mother's house with your bag of dirty clothes in one hand and a pail of chalk in the other. She's painted the house again, some time ago by the looks of it. She tried to go with green, probably in an attempt to match the colour of the needles from the pine tree that once stood in the front yard, but the colour, either poorly chosen or poorly applied, just makes the house look like it's moulding. The stump from the old tree is still there. It's grey now, but you remember that it looked orange when it was first cut down. You used to jump up and down on it until the bottoms of your shoes were covered in sap and your feet became glued to the kitchen floor when you went inside. Yesterday is the past and tomorrow is uncertain. You read that once on the wall above a urinal in a men's room in a bar. It feels incomplete. Where does the present fit into that phrase that you read above a urinal? You walk toward the front door, taking a step toward yesterday and tomorrow, all in the present.

Where is your bag? is the first thing your mother asks when she opens the door.

I lost it, you tell her.

It's a good thing you wore something nice, she says, not noticing the tags still hanging down from your shirt sleeve. You put the pail of chalk down by the door and raise your free arm, but your mother turns away and disappears into the kitchen. If you were to close your eyes and just breathe in the air, you could swear that you were coming home from your first day of school, and the scene would have been much the same, so you decide to keep your eyes open the entire time you are in the house so as not to be fooled by nostalgia triggered by familiar smells. In the kitchen, your mother sits at the table, a jigsaw puzzle piece hovering over a half-finished puzzle of a lighthouse. You ask her where the scissors are and she looks up from the puzzle piece as though she is surprised to see you standing in her kitchen. You find the scissors in the same drawer they were always in and cut the tags from your clothes and put them in your pocket. You sit across from your mother and pick up a puzzle piece.

You're going to mess it all up, she says, taking the piece from you and putting it back down in the exact same place you found it. I have a system. A very precise system.

She microwaves two frozen dinners and you sit in the living room with the lights off and the TV on. There is a story on the news about a small commuter plane that has gone missing somewhere in the mountains of Indonesia.

How was your flight? your mother asks.

It was fine.

I wish you kids didn't have to fly all over the country like you do. You'll never get me on a plane, no sir, no sir, you'll never get me on a plane. They are nothing but deathtraps.

You scrape the plastic bottom of your frozen-dinner tray and rinse it out in the sink, and following your mother's precise instructions, place it with the others in the cupboard below where you find more stacks of frozen-dinner trays, cups from fast food restaurants, and straws stacked neatly beside them. It's just like when your father left and your mother developed a habit of not throwing anything away. Everything has a use, she used to say, and you never know when you might need something. You pour milk into an old McDonald's cup and sip it through a straw while watching the nightly weather report. Your mother holds a book in her hands but it's too dark to read and you notice that she is holding it upside down anyway.

How's Marie and the baby? you ask. She puts the book down, first marking her page with a piece of string, and she tells you that Marie lost the baby.

You never answer your phone, you never listen to my messages, you are just so involved in your own goddamned life that you don't care about anybody but yourself.

As she talks, her voice shrinking, you picture your answering machine in your apartment, the red light blinking with a message from your mother about the death of Marie's baby, waiting for you to hit play when you get back home.

Where's Marie now? you ask.

She's upstairs in her room.

You knock on Marie's door, but there's no answer. Just go in, your mother says, opening the door herself and stepping into the dark room. In the light from the hallway, you see Marie lying on the bed facing away from the door. You walk around to the other side and your mother turns on a light on the night stand. Marie's eyes are wide open and stare out blankly at the wall, just like the stare of Franklin's lost men buried and then exhumed in the Arctic. Marie, there's someone here to see you, your mother says, but Marie does not move or even shift her eyes to look at you. Your mother sits on the bed, strokes Marie's hair, and after wiping only the first tear, she allows the others to roll down her cheek and fall to the bed. This is what pain looks like, you think. This is sadness. You are grateful to be a witness to it because you can feel the electricity in the air, which grounds you firmly to the surface of the earth, and when you try to move away you cannot because it feels like your shoes are glued to the floor.

YOU SIT ON the end of the bed in your old room. There is a sewing machine in the corner that your mother moved into the room the day after you moved out, but it looks like it hasn't been used since. The walls are bare, the top of the dresser clear, just like it was when you lived here. But when you open the drawers of the dresser, you find old receipts for frozen dinners, books, wine, coffee, lawn ornaments. In other drawers there are empty pill bottles, roles of undeveloped film, balled-up string, dead pens, full and empty notepads, and other things that are still awaiting their day to be useful again. On the wall just beside the light switch, you can still see the dull spot in the paint where the oil from your forehead left its mark. There are other dark smudges on the wall, old fingerprints, and you place your hand over top of your little hand that would run up and down the wall as you pressed your forehead into the paint and listened to your parents fighting downstairs through a crack in the door. After it was all finished, when the yelling either gave way to sobs or just silence, your father would come stomping up the stairs, the entire house groaning under his rage, and you would watch him with an eye peeking out from behind the door as he walked past your room and locked himself in the bathroom. He would sit on the toilet for hours, smoking cigarette after cigarette, and drinking beer that he kept in an inch of cold water in the tub. You used to play with the empty cans when you bathed, filling them with water and pouring them over your head, and you would go to school the next day smelling of beer and stale cigarette smoke.

Sometimes after the shouting downstairs stopped and your father gave up trying to find any particular usefulness for your mother, he came upstairs and spotted you looking out from behind your bedroom door. He burst through, knocking you backward and onto the floor, and accused you of spying. Everyone was against him. He didn't have a friend in the world. He lifted you up by the arm and threw you into bed, tossing the covers every which way, tucking them between your legs and under your arms, until you were a twisted mess of blankets and limbs. Go to sleep, he shouted, and then slammed the door, taking his place on the closed toilet seat to smoke and weep. You stayed twisted up in the sheets the entire night, even though you had to go to the bathroom. You didn't dare move or use the cup you hid under your bed for when you had to pee in the night, so you just peed in the mangled mess of sheets. No one noticed, and because the sheets were such a mess when you went that night, you had no way of knowing where you peed, being too afraid to look the next morning before school. So for the next several weeks, when you went to bed, you twisted, spun, rolled, and bounced in the sheets, and tied yourself up into one giant knot, not knowing or caring what part of the sheet was wrapped around your face that night.

THE TV IS still on when you wake up on the couch. Your mother is sitting in the chair across from you, watching the static on the screen. It's three in the morning. She asks you about your girlfriend. Sitting up and tossing the blanket from your legs, you tell your mother that she is fine because you can't bring yourself to tell her that she broke up with you almost a year ago.

When are you going to get married and start a family? You know that I'm not getting any younger.

I don't know if that's something you need to worry about, you tell her.

You turn off the TV and lie back down in the dark room. Your mother continues to sit there in the dark, mourning the loss of yet another grandchild.

When you leave the next morning, you take the pail of chalk that you left by the front door. You place it in the trunk of your mother's car because when she saw it by the door she cried. You drive into town and spend the day aimlessly following familiar roads from your childhood and take note of the buildings that have been torn down and the fire hydrants that are painted red now instead of yellow. You stop at a bar and spin in circles on the bar stool. There is a woman dancing on top of a table in her bare feet and the entire scene looks so much more depressing with the daylight still casting shadows on the far wall. You ask the bartender, a middle-aged woman with frizzy hair, why the fire hydrants are red now. The creases around her eyes cut through the black circles underneath as she tries to figure you out. I'm just curious to know what goes into making a decision like that, you say. Was the town consulted or was it just a decision made by the fire department? She looks past you, at the dancing woman, and calls to her to get down before she slips and breaks her neck. You spin back around and watch the woman peel her feet from the surface of the table, and when she bends down to search out a chair with her bare foot, her dress rides up so you can see her underwear, an unflattering, white, pastel-green floral pattern.

You order another drink and take the change the bartender lays out and call your girlfriend from the pay phone by the bathrooms. You tell her about Marie and the baby and she asks you if there is anything she can do. It's okay, you tell her. Then you tell her that you ran into an old friend from high school. That's good, you should get together to catch up. It might help take your mind off things. You mention the dancing woman's underwear and she tells you that she has to get going.

She hangs up and the line goes dead. You keep standing there with the phone to your ear and start punching in the phone numbers of various people you know because you like the feeling of pay phone buttons and how far in they can be pushed. The dancing woman walks past you and goes into the women's bathroom. You can hear her coughing, or heaving, or possibly throwing up and you lean back to see if it's dark yet, but light still cuts into the darkness of the bar.

When she comes out you notice that she still isn't wearing any shoes and black lines from her eye makeup run down from the corner of each eye. With the phone still pressed to your ear you tell her that she missed a spot. She sucks in her bottom lip and looks far more alert than she did before. Don't worry, you say, it will be dark soon. The woman grabs the phone from your hand and smacks you on the ear with it. You crumble down against the wall and she tries to hit you again but the cord keeps the receiver from smacking you on the ear a second time. She throws the receiver down when she is pulled away by the man she was dancing for at the table. As soon as it becomes dark, the couple, who had been sitting in silence mostly, leave and you ask the bartender about the dancing woman.

She's a regular, the bartender says.

A regular what?

A regular train wreck.

You light a cigarette in your mother's car without thinking and now you have to keep driving around to air out the inside. You stop in the empty parking lot of the department store where you bought the lavender shirt that you are currently wearing and run your hands over the seats and check the floor mats to make sure that you didn't leave any ash behind. You sit on the hood of the car under a white lamp, smoking, and listening to the flutter of moth wings circling the bulb overhead. You flick the cigarette butt to the side and start to cry for Marie's baby, the baby you never met, and all the children you will never meet. You take the pail of chalk from the trunk, it's little white handle and colourful graphics seeming so sad now. Inside are a couple dozen thick, colourful pieces of chalk that rattle around and you find a blue one. You sit in front of the car next to the concrete base of the lamppost and you wonder what name Marie had given her baby. You never thought to ask and it's too late now. In the empty parking space you write out all the names you can think of in blue chalk. You fill two empty parking spaces with names for boys and girls. You stand and look at all the names under the white light and you think that maybe the name is there somewhere. It probably is because you're sure that Marie had mentioned it to you in the past, you just can't remember, or you were just too involved in your own goddamned life to listen. You cradle the piece of blue chalk in your palm, the end now rounded from scribbling out so many names on the asphalt, and you are thankful that the pail of chalk did not go to waste. You throw the blue piece down as hard as you can and it explodes in a cloud of blue dust that drifts across the parking lot and then you put the pail back in the trunk. On the way back to your mother's house you stop at the bridge crossing the river and hang over the side. You can't see the water and it's like staring down into a bottomless pit and you wonder what it would feel like to fall forever.

IN THE LIGHT from the static of the TV, you see that your mother is holding a book right-side up and is drinking wine from a Styrofoam cup. You sit across from her and comment on the new fire hydrants. Were you part of that decision? you ask. Don't be a smartass, she says. She puts her book down and turns the channel on the TV and ends up on a nature show about alligators. You mention that you saw this already and she tosses you the remote and tells you to watch whatever you want, but you leave it on the alligator show. The room is silent, broken only by the sound of an alligator splashing in a swamp or more wine being added to the Styrofoam cup. Little has changed since you were young. The room was always bathed in the glow from the TV and someone was usually drunk or getting drunk. Marie would be sitting on the floor, brushing the hair of her Barbie doll with a small, pink plastic brush, while your mother sat in the same chair reading the same book. You would tell ghost stories about how children disappeared in the woods behind the school and your mother would tell you to stop being stupid and scaring Marie. This was after your father left. When he was still there, it was very much the same, only there was the possibility of more exciting things to come, which often came on cue.

You're such a pig, your father would announce out of nowhere.

Would you shut your goddamn mouth, your mother would reply.

A shadow moved across the white glow on the wall of the living room as your mother crossed the floor to slap your father across the face. More words, more slaps, then your father locked in the upstairs bathroom and your mother banging on the door for hours. Marie kept brushing her doll's hair, harder and harder, until tufts of hair were pulled out by that little plastic brush and became woven into the fibres of the carpet.

THE ELECTRICITY HAS faded and Marie's room feels dull, empty. Your mother sits at the bedside while Marie remains frozen in her childhood bed. Friends of hers come and go, each offering their own suggestions for coaxing her out of bed, but nothing seems to work. You keep them company in the living room after they give up. They ask you what it's like living in the big city and you say that it's dirty. They assure you that Marie will bounce back; she just needs time to come to terms with what's happened. Marie's oldest friend arrives with her five-year-old son and asks you to watch him while she checks in on Marie. The boy runs a toy car over the coffee table, leaving scuff marks in the wood. You stare at him from the couch, never knowing what to say to children, and he runs the car from the coffee table, to the couch, and over your knees.

Oh my goodness, your mother cries when she comes into the room. Why did you let him do that?

It's just a coffee table, you say, looking at the water rings and scratches pockmarking the wood.

It's my coffee table.

She takes hold of the boy and slaps him on the behind and he begins to cry, bringing his mother running down the stairs to hoist him up into her arms and give you and your mother a dirty look. The child's cries echo throughout the house as she takes him to the door and your mother tells her that it wasn't wise to bring him here and that she should know better.

YOU CALL THE number on the piece of paper with the smiley face and set a time to meet the tattooed cashier from the department store. When you walk into the restaurant, you find her sitting in a booth near the back flanked by two fair-haired children. She tells you all about her life without any prompting. She goes into great detail about her children's fathers and why she left them. The struggles of a single mother seem unending. You listen politely, while silently wishing that you had taken the pills prescribed to you for flying before coming, and when she finally asks about you, you tell her that you can't remember her name. She laughs and slaps your hand from across the table and says that you've always been a joker. But you really can't and you only have vague memories of this woman from high school. Her son, four years old, tugs on her shirt sleeve, and asks for more milk.

That shirt is a good colour for you, she says. Your wife will love it.

I'm not married.

Your girlfriend?

No.

Oh, that's a shame.

I want more milk, mommy.

How long are you in town for?

Not long.

Milk.

Will you be coming back again soon?

I don't know.

Well, I hope we can get together again before you leave.

I'm pretty busy.

Mommy, I want more milk.

Fuck, can't you see mommy is talking? Keep your fucking mouth shut. I'll ask for more milk when the waitress comes back.

The struggle is never-ending, you think. You offer to pay for the meal and she is grateful. She offers to make you coffee at her house but you decline. She hugs you before you can leave and her children wrap around your legs, their little hands pulling on the back of your pant leg. As soon as you are able to break free, you run out the door and get into your mother's car. You never want to see a child ever again, nor the people who have them.

THE SKY IS criss-crossed with vapour trails left behind by planes flying overhead. You spot two in the sky and it looks like they are headed for each other. As they get closer, you brace yourself for the deaths of hundreds of people, but the planes cross paths, their white trails making a giant X in the sky. Your mother comes outside and catches you smoking and lectures you about killing yourself. Then she demands her car keys, saying that she can't take it anymore, that she has to get out of this bloody house. Why don't I ever get what I want? she says, looking to you for a sincere answer, but you say nothing. She looks down at the smoking cigarette at your feet and shakes her head and walks back inside. You feel as small as your six-year-old self, caught in the backyard trying to hit songbirds with a slingshot. Why would you want to hurt something so beautiful?

You soak your shirt and pants in the sink, the dark stains from the bus floor turning the water nearly black. As you ring the shirt out, Marie appears next to you at the sink. She dips her hands into the water and squeezes a pant leg and asks how your clothes got so dirty. I fell on the bus, you say. The pant leg slaps back down into the water and she braces herself against the edge of the sink, her head hanging down. You keep your hands under the black water and stare out the window at the songbirds congregating in the apple tree in the backyard.

I'm empty, Marie says, I have nothing left. You tell her that you're sorry and nothing more. Marie stands back up and leans against the counter. Her small frame looks so frail, with the exception of the small bump on her stomach, which she cradles with her thin arms. I just want to die, she says. You lift the stopper out of the sink and it gurgles as it swallows up the black water. You have a similar, silent feeling in your throat as you swallow back what feels like the most significant crying fit you could ever experience.

You don't have to stay, you know.

I know, you say. I have to be back at work next week.

She wraps an arm around you and rests her head on your shoulder. You lie and tell her that everything will be all right. She slides free from your body and stands in the middle of the kitchen. You can see her reflection in the window.

If you ever come back and I'm gone... She loses the rest of the words, which are just as inconceivable to say as they are to think.

She turns around and leaves the kitchen. You watch her reflection disappear from the window and think that she's gone already.

YOUR MOTHER IS asleep in the chair with the TV on. As a child you were surrounded by the constant ticking of clocks, each room containing at least one. But now there is no ticking and it's unsettling how silent a house can become. You take the pail of chalk from your mother's car and walk to the basement. You take out a piece of white chalk and lie down on the cold cement floor that looks white in the light from the moon. You trace out an outline of your body on the floor, arms out stretched, feet shoulder width apart, and you stay there for a long time. When you stand up, you look down at the empty outline of your body on the cement floor. This is what it looks like, you think, to be empty. You sit in an old folding chair and watch as the moonlight travels across the floor, overtaking your hollow body, swallowing the lines in its white light, and try to understand what exactly Marie is feeling.

You help your mother wash another set of frozen-dinner trays and place them in the cupboard with the rest. She asks about your girlfriend again and says that she always loved her. Then she pauses, her hands absently searching through the soapy water for another disposable cup. She tells you to get married and start a family. Don't go through life alone, she says. You notice that your mother's hands are shaking and you ask her if she is taking her medication. Don't get smart with me, she says. That'll be the day that you start getting on my case about medication and thinking you know what's best for me. You rinse a Styrofoam cup and hand it to her to dry. She notices a crack in the side and throws it in the garbage while blaming you for ruining her things.

You go to Marie's room before leaving and you kneel down next to the bed. She stares at you, just like before, not moving, her eyes blank. I have to go now, you tell her. You hope to see at least some kind of reaction, to know that you didn't dream her appearing next to the sink the day before. But she gives you nothing. You tell her that you look forward to seeing her again and that you want her to be here when you come back. But before leaving, you tell her that you will understand. She closes her eyes and doesn't open them again. You leave the room and close the door. Your mother is sitting at the table, still working on the same puzzle of the lighthouse. You stand over the table, looking at the incomplete picture, while discreetly shuffling around pieces in the bottom of the box.

I have to go now, you say.
Okay.
I'm sorry that things couldn't have been different.
It is what it is. We'll be fine. Always have been.
The struggle is never-ending.
What was that?

Nothing.

You fill one of your mother's McDonald's cups with water and seal the lid with the straw poking out. You take a sip and say goodbye, but your mother doesn't say anything. Just before you can leave the kitchen, she calls to you, and asks if you touched her puzzle pieces. No, you say, and you take the plastic bag with your clothes and the pail of chalk and walk out the front door, leaving behind your silhouette on the basement floor to go along with the smudge of your forehead and fingerprints on the bedroom wall.

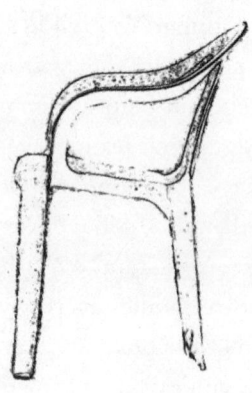

III

Chalk Lines

The familiar drone of the ringing phone resonates in your ear. One, two, three. Come on, pick up. You hold the receiver so close to your face that your lips touch it, like a kiss between you and all the other punks and drunks that have stumbled into this little piece of paradise and have used the phone to call drug dealers, prostitutes, and mothers. You pull away, spitting to the side, when your girlfriend picks up.

I can't get back on that plane, you say.

What happened?

I just can't do it. I can't get back on that plane.

How are you going to get back home?

I don't know.

You're more likely to die...

I know, I know, I'm more likely to die on the way to the airport.

There's a pause, broken only by the sound of shattering glass. Did you just break a plate? you ask.

I think that was on your end.

Your girlfriend says something but you are distracted by the sound of glass scraping along a tile floor behind the swinging brown doors down the hall from the pay phones.

What?

I said, How's Marie?

She's been better.

Can she get through this?

I don't know.

There is another pause. You could take a bus, your girlfriend suggests.

I could. Just as long as it's not headed toward any airports.

ON THE WAY to the bus station, you spot a black suitcase leaning against a building. You pull the cord and jump off the bus and you see that there is a piece of red yarn tied to the handle. The suitcase flops open when you grab it and everything inside is gone. You place your plastic bag with your shirt and pants and the pail of chalk inside and zip it back up. When the next bus comes, you ask the driver how to get to the bus station, and he tells you to get back on the crosstown route.

At the bus station, you feed quarters into a small TV attached to the chair and watch a show about how rivets are made. You run out of change before discovering the final step in the process and you ask the person next to you if he knows how rivets are made. You sit next to the window near the back of the bus, glad to see the ground just outside the window and to know that you won't be leaving it. You contemplate taking some of your pills anyway so you can sleep the entire way, but you don't want to wake up on the floor in the middle of the aisle and ruin your new lavender shirt. Someone takes the seat next to you. You cannot tell if it is a man or a woman. He or she wears a heavy-knit hat, a tattered green jacket that looks army surplus, and Doc Martens. The bag on his or her lap is covered with buttons of bands you've never heard of and safety pins, and looks heavy. As the bus pulls away from the station, you rest your head on the glass and watch the red fire hydrants go past, thankful that you are leaving this place with its wrong-coloured fire hydrants.

A man and a woman two rows up from you argue loudly about money and commitment and then space and time, but not in a Carl Sagan way. Your seat mate tells them to shut the fuck up, and the entire bus goes silent for a moment, as heads turn to try to figure out where the effeminately masculine voice came from, but the chatter soon starts up again and the man and woman pick up where they left off.

I fucking hate the bus, he or she says. Where you going?

Home.

And where is home?

You sort of shrug and shake your head, as though going home was more of an abstract thought than a real destination, because you could argue that you are leaving home, too.

I get it.

Where are you going?

He or she points to the front of the bus. That way.

You examine this person's face when you are able to steal a glance. The lips are thin and very pink in colour. There are freckles under the eyes and you spot an earring under the heavy-knit hat. Any strands of hair that escape look to be red in colour, almost orange. The hands look large, not quite as large as your own, but big enough to be a man's. An hour into the trip, you are still going over in your head whether or not this person is a man or a woman. It doesn't really matter, it's a distraction more than anything, like trying to figure out if someone who's staring at you from across a room is thinking about you or merely lost in a daydream, but it gets to the point where it is all you can think about. So finally you turn to your seat mate and say, excuse me, but you are cut off when a hand is extended and you are introduced to L.

Is that short for anything? you ask.

No, just L, and your seat mate draws a vertical line in the air, followed by a horizontal one, a capital L.

L rifles through the bag on L's lap and pulls out a tube of cherry Chap Stick. L offers you some but you tell L that you make a point of not touching people on buses. L laughs and says you are being smart because most people that ride buses are dirty punks. At the first stop, you stand on the side of the highway and smoke a cigarette. L asks to bum a smoke and you give her one. She sits cross-legged on the gravel, and the way she squints her eyes to look up at you in the sun, you see how fine her features are and you think that L must be a woman. You sit next to her and toss small stones at the back tire of the bus. The ones that miss the rubber clink in the chrome hub and you ask L if she knows how rivets are made. Can't say that I do, she says.

Back on the bus, the arguing couple are now making out, louder than when they were yelling at one another. L shakes her head and leans in toward you and says that people have no decency anymore.

Last night, at the bus station, I saw two guys going at it in the men's room. They couldn't even be bothered to step into a stall, just right there in front of the sink. L leans back and puts his knees on the seat in front of him.

Did you know them? you ask.

Who?

The two men in the men's room.

Fuck no, why would I know them? Do you think I live at the bus station or something? That's a bit of a snap judgment.

That's not what I meant. I just thought, it's a small town, everyone knows everyone else.

I'm not from there. I was just passing through that shit hole.

Where are you from?

L points to the front of the bus again and says, everywhere and nowhere.

You turn away and look back at the telephone poles passing by along the side of the highway. You are driving down the roads that cut through the empty fields you saw from the sky and you keep watch for the little white houses. As soon as you spot one, you look up at the sky for any vapour trails, but there are only grey clouds.

You know what, fuck you, L says, sitting back up straight. I can't believe you thought I was some kind of bum living in a bus station. Do you think I hang around in men's bathrooms hoping to suck some guy off for spare change? Is that what you think of me? L is becoming as loud as the arguing couple she had told to shut up, and even *they* stop sucking the spit from each other's mouths to listen to the tirade coming from two rows back.

I didn't think that at all, you say with your hands up.

Whatever, L says, getting up from his seat but leaving his bag. After several minutes you look over the top of your seat and see that the bathroom door is still closed. You lift the corner flap on the bag but drop it back down when you hear the bathroom door open. L returns, slumps back in his seat, and pulls at the loose threads from a tear in the knee of his jeans.

During the second stop, you sit at a picnic table with your head in your hands. It feels like you haven't slept in days. The cigarette between your fingers burns down until it touches your skin and you flick it away. L, who has been lingering near the road, approaches and sits across from you on the bench and asks to bum another cigarette. I'm all out, you say. He nods and starts searching through his bag again.

I'm sorry for losing my shit earlier, L says. I just get a little sensitive about some things. You tell him not to worry about it and hand him a cigarette and walk back to the bus.

You rest your head against the window and try to sleep. You wish that it would start raining so you could watch the water stream across the glass and focus on something moving slowly. You try to think about what's waiting for you back in the city, but nothing comes to mind, just like nothing is waiting for you in the small town you just left, the town you grew up in. It seems the only place you belong is in the space between, in constant transition, nowhere. You crave another cigarette and ask L how much longer until the next stop. Another hour, L says, maybe less. You close your eyes again, and when you press your face to the glass, there is a loud bang and the bus swerves back and forth. There are screams and the sound of breaking glass, and finally everything comes to a sudden stop. You turn to L and ask if the bus was headed to the airport.

THE FRONT OF the bus is smashed in and the remains of a cow lay spread out on the highway. The passengers are boarded into a school bus that takes you to a small town ten kilometres down the road where you are told that another bus won't be able to come until the next day. Standing outside of a roadside motel, you see L by the highway, her thumb in the air. You ask him what he is doing and she tells you that she isn't waiting around for some other bus that probably won't even come. Is there someplace you need to be? you ask, but L doesn't answer. A pickup truck pulls up on the side of the road and L runs to the passenger side window and talks to the driver. She then turns to you and asks if you want to come. She gets in the truck and leaves the door open, so you lift your nearly empty suitcase into the back of the truck and get in.

A giant black dog crosses L's legs and lies down across your lap. The old man behind the wheel with smooth skin pulled back over high cheekbones introduces you to Colonel Admiral and assures you that he is a first-class gentleman. The driver tells you that he will take you and L as far as the next town, but no further. It's closer than we were before, L says. The radio is on and tuned to what sounds like an automated disaster response station, with a monotone voice repeating wind speeds, atmospheric pressure, and moisture levels in the air.

It's for the pilots at the airfield, the driver says. They dust crops and need to know these things.

Are you a pilot? L asks.

Me? No. I'm legally blind in my left eye. It was from an accident when I was a boy. A car battery exploded. My son, he flies.

As L and the driver talk about airplane tires clipping the tops of corn stalks and the likelihood of car battery explosions in modern cars, you sit still with your hands by your chest and away from Colonel Admiral, whose entire body shakes as he pants. Drool drips from his tongue and covers the armrest and door handle. The smell of his breath is overpowering. L offers the driver her tube of Chap Stick after applying another coat to his lips. The driver takes the tube, smells it, and hands it back, saying that he doesn't care for the taste of cherry.

You pull into a gas station after driving for thirty minutes and you forget about the drool on the handle when you open the door. Colonel Admiral doesn't move, and when you try to push him off your burning lap, he looks up at you with his brown eyes and growls. The driver whistles and the dog jumps from your lap, scratching your inner thigh with his final leap. Good luck to you, the driver says. L lifts your suitcase out of the back and picks it up and down off the ground, testing its weight.

Wait, this is it? This is the next town?

Uh huh, the driver says. Come Colonel, then the driver disappears into the diner and you look back to L.

You're travelling light, she says, handing you the suitcase.

You sit in a booth by the window and watch as L tears open sugar packets and pours the contents onto the table, adding to an ever-growing white mountain. You order eggs and toast, and L, a basket of french fries. Well, what do we do now? you ask. L presses her finger down into the mountain of sugar and small avalanches of grains go tumbling down from the top and spread out across the corner of the table.

I didn't know that we were a *we*, L says.

You asked me to come.

I didn't make you. Why did you come?

Because you asked me.

The waitress returns and refills your coffee cup. How far is the next town? L asks.

Thirty kilometres west, the waitress says.

Is there somewhere to rent a car in town? you ask.

No, nothing like that. You might be able to hitch a ride, though there ain't much traffic on the highway this time of day.

Maybe we can get Colonel Admiral to take us back to the motel and wait for the bus, you say.

That would be going backward, L says, dipping the end of a fry into the jam on your toast. You see Colonel Admiral jumping back into the truck and you announce that there's still time to catch him. You lick the jam from the end of your finger and realize then that you forgot to wash your hands. You sit back down in the booth, your hand held in the air like a one-armed surgeon, and finish the rest of your breakfast at four in the afternoon, but the lingering taste of Colonel Admiral's breath will be with you for the rest of the day.

YOU RENT THE last room at a roadside motel across the street from the diner. You strip the sheets from the bed and L watches from her own and asks you what you're doing.

I'm checking for bugs, you tell her.

Bugs?

Bedbugs.

I thought those were a myth.

You run your hands over the bare mattress, leaning down to look in every crease and valley in the springs. Do you have any change for the TV? L asks, bouncing off the end of her bed and twisting around the antenna. You watch *America's Funniest Home Videos* and neither you nor L laugh along with the studio audience. L lights one of your cigarettes and you ask her what she's doing.

Sorry, can I bum a smoke?

No, not that, go outside.

Outside?

To smoke, don't smoke in here.

What does it matter?

I don't like the smell. You grab the pack and step outside and L follows.

Do you think there's a bar in this town? you think aloud. Let's go find one. L knocks on every door of the motel until someone finally answers and you are pointed to a street behind the gas station. The bar looks like all the other two-storey houses that line the street, the only difference being that all the windows are lit up, even the top one, which isn't so much a window, but a vent for the attic. The bar is in fact someone's house and you and L take a table in a small upstairs bedroom, which only has two tables, so close together that you have to slide your butt over the opposite one to fit through the space. The waitress asks L for ID and she searches through her bag, but comes back with nothing, saying that she must have lost it during the bus accident. You tell the waitress that it's true, we were in a bus accident. Sorry, sweetie, I can't serve you if you don't have any ID. You order a beer with a glass and pour half for L.

On the wall over L's shoulder there is a collection of stickers of Rainbow Brite ponies and Strawberry Shortcake. Someone tried to peel some off, but they only tore the paper away, leaving the gluey back still stuck to the wall. It's depressing. L says that she grew up in a bedroom just like this, with the sloping ceiling and beige-coloured walls.

Did you like Rainbow Brite? you ask.

What the fuck is that?

You point to the stickers behind her and he turns around and says fuck no.

Drinking half a beer at a time is slow, tedious work, but you persevere. A heavy-set woman and a skinny man with a narrow moustache enter the room and the man is able to slither between the tables and sit down beside you. The woman takes up nearly the entire entrance with her body and you lean to the window and wonder how far it is to the ground in case there's a fire and you have to jump.

So what do you do? you ask L. Are you a student? A cashier? Do you hang around men's rooms at bus stations? L examines her fingernail that was just between his teeth and tells you that you're funny.

So what do you do?

I get by.

Doing what?

Whatever I have to.

Do you live on the streets?

What's it to you?

The little man beside you lights a cigarette and soon the small room fills with smoke. L, seeing this, looks to you and you slide the pack across the table to him. You open the window to let the smoke out and light your own. The little room starts spinning the moment the smoke hits your lungs and you hang your head out the window because you feel like you are about to throw up. Below you is the roof of a shed or garage with rain gutters, so if you do get sick, you take comfort in knowing it will be taken care of properly.

After L finishes the beer left in his glass, her eyes start to droop and she is the quietest he's been since you met her. You suspect that she is drunk so you decide to drink the next bottle of beer all to yourself, and L doesn't seem to mind. You hear people shouting downstairs and outside. A bottle is broken. It sounds like the people next to you are playing patty cake. You take the burning cigarette from between L's fingers and drop it into your beer bottle. The little room starts to get smaller, the sounds of hands slapping and people shouting growing louder. You ask L if she's all right and he lifts her head off the table, his eyes closing one at a time in a desperate attempt to stay awake. L, are you a man or a woman? you ask. L smiles, laughter building silently in his chest. Then she leans forward, eyes suddenly wide open, and says, I'm L, what more do you need to know? And in that moment you admire L, and you fall in love a little bit, with the things that you know and even more so with the things that you don't.

You tell L about Marie and her baby. You tell L about going back home and how nothing is waiting for you there. You tell L about your girlfriend and what it's like to be in love when you have a broken heart. L listens with her head on the table and nods occasionally, sometimes sitting back up and taking a drag from the cigarette left smoking in the ashtray that you share with him.

Is your girlfriend waiting for you back home? L asks.//
I told you that nothing is waiting for me back home.
Not even her?
I don't know. Maybe. I think she's engaged.
Are you delusional?
That's a bit of a snap judgement.
You sound delusional to me.

That's because you've never been in love.

I thought that love was a myth.

It is like bedbugs, it really gets under your skin.

You order another beer and you tell L to sit up straight before the waitress comes. The waitress arrives and sees L sitting up, her head rolling around on her shoulders. Has she been drinking? the waitress asks. Not to my knowledge, you say. She's really tired. The bus accident and all. Very traumatic. Though she would like some water. The waitress looks to the other two in the room, but they say nothing. You nod in thanks to them and the woman smiles at you. You notice then that she too has a moustache, a very faint moustache, fine, and you imagine very soft.

You encourage L to drink the water, which she does, tipping the glass back and draining it all. After you smoke another cigarette, you have to put your head on the table, too. It feels cold against your ear and you can hear your heartbeat. You can hear the voices of the people below you, or beside you, or two rows in front of you, and the drone of the bus engine. They argue about money and commitment and space and time, but not in the Carl Sagan way. They yell at each other about distance and weakness. You're just so pathetic, she says, I'm just tired of being the one to do everything.

I'm doing my best, you say.

How many times are you going to say that? Nothing has changed.

I can change.

You say that all the time too, and nothing has changed.

Just give me a chance.

How many chances can I give you? I'm just so tired.

Your head shoots up off the table and L stares at you, her eyes wide open, a gentle smile on his lips. You turn to the couple beside you and shout, will you two shut up already? They don't even turn to acknowledge you, so you slap their table and say, enough. The woman waves her arms in the air, then the man follows suit, the cigarettes they hold like little flaming batons. They sign at you and then to one another, their blurry hands cutting through the thick smoke. You sit back and start to laugh and they stop signing. You lean in close to their table and say, that's right, I said shut up. The man stands and throws a glass of gin all over your lavender shirt. You try to splash what's left of your beer onto him, but it only dribbles out of the mouth of the bottle and down your pant leg. He takes a step toward you and, in a moment of panic, not unlike being on an airplane that suddenly drops, you turn around and squeeze your body through the small opening in the window and land on the roof of the shed. You turn and roll off the edge and land on the dirt path below.

You wake up to someone rifling through your pockets. You see L standing over you, feeling your butt and finding your wallet. Are you robbing me? you ask. I have to pay the fucking tab, you idiot. A small crowd has gathered around the path and you hear someone say that you jumped out the window. On purpose? What a fucking loser. As you lay on the ground waiting for the people to go away and for L to return, a dog comes up and starts licking your face. The familiar taste of Colonel Admiral's breath hits your tongue and you tell him to fuck off. He growls at you, then disappears amongst the legs of the crowd that has grown and is now laughing at some joke, most likely at your expense. L comes back and helps you to your feet. She tells you to wipe your face, and when you do, you smear wet dirt across your cheek and you ask L if you were crying. She doesn't answer and you push through the crowd and stumble back down the road lined with white houses. You suggest trying a different one, but all the lights are out, all the other bars in this town are closed.

You both fall in the middle of the highway in front of the gas station. If there were a bus, you would end up like the cow that is probably still spread out on the highway just beyond the next town over. Lucky bastard, you say. L helps you onto the bed and you say that you need to wash your lavender shirt because it has gin on it. You turn on the shower and run your head under the water, but you don't take off your shirt. When you come back into the room, L is sitting on the bed and chewing on her fingernails. His green jacket is missing, along with her heavy-knit hat, and she wears a red plaid shirt. His hair is short and orange at the tips, leading into blonde along the sides, and eventually becoming brown at the roots. You stand at the end of her bed trying to detect any sign of breasts. You're scaring me, she says. You apologize and lie down on your bed. You search through your pockets for change but notice that your wallet is gone. Do you have my wallet? L tosses it to you and you announce that there will be no *America's Funniest*

Home Videos tonight because you don't have any change. L sits on the edge of the bed, staring at you, and says, you're not planning on fucking me, are you? It hadn't occurred to me, you say, rolling away to the other side. You pick up the phone and try to call your girlfriend. Your lips kiss the receiver as the ringing drones in your ear. I'm sorry, your call cannot be completed as dialed. Please hang up and try your call again. This is a recording.

You fall asleep to the sound of running water and you dream that your body dissolves in the rain, so you can never go outside, even on a clear day, because there's always a chance the sky will cloud over and you won't be able to outrun a storm. In the dream you are standing on a porch, watching the rain. You are tempted to hold out your hand, trying to imagine the feeling of the water hitting your skin. The house is leaking again, streams of water pour down from the ceiling and you have to tiptoe around the pools on the floor. Your girlfriend is sitting at the kitchen table licking raspberry jam from a spoon. Or maybe she's your wife. A broken plate lies scattered on the green tile floor. You sit down across from her between two falling streams of water. You tell her that you love her. I'm sorry, she says, placing the spoon on the table, your call cannot be completed as dialed. Please hang up and try your call again.

The light is still on when you wake up and the water is still running. L is gone. Your head is pounding and your mouth feels like an ashtray full of dirt and beer, with hints of Colonel Admiral. You step outside for a cigarette, and as you sit in the round plastic chair beside the door looking out at the highway, you see a Greyhound bus fly past. You sip water from the bathroom sink and splash some over your face. You pull back the shower curtain to turn off the water and find L standing there naked. And now you know.

ANOTHER CAR DRIVES past without stopping. L lowers her thumb and continues walking along the side of the highway, you following, pulling your nearly empty suitcase behind. Grasshoppers jump from your path and click their wings in the tall grass in protest. You have to stop again to throw up in the ditch and ask L if she has any more water. A transport truck comes over the hill, and when it drives past, a wave of hot air blows into your face and you feel like you might pass out.

You know that it's you, right? you say to L, who is throwing small stones at a speed-limit sign.

Excuse me?

That's why no one is stopping, because of you. Maybe you should hide in the grass and then come out when I get a car to stop.

L starts laughing.

Look at you, she says. With your gin-stained lavender shirt, pressed slacks, and suitcase. You're the one who looks like a fucking murderer. What kind of person dressed like that hitches a ride on a highway? I'm standard. I'm the norm. No one is stopping because of you and your ugly shirt.

What did you say?

I said your shirt is ugly. You look terrible in that colour.

You push the handle of your suitcase in, leave it on the side of the highway, and take two large steps toward L and her pinched lips and narrowed eyes.

Well, at least I don't look like a boy, you say. Fuck.

YOU BOTH STAND in the shade of a highway sign, which informs you that the next town is still fourteen kilometres away. L asks for a cigarette and you pull the pack from your shirt pocket. The piece of paper with the phone number and smiley face on it falls out and L steps on it to keep it from blowing down the highway. You pull out your last cigarette and tell L that it will have to be shared. Is this your new girlfriend's number? she asks, holding up the piece of paper. You tell her that it is the number of a cashier at a department store who is thirty-two years old and still goes to high school and is trying to raise two bratty children on her own, and that she is the epitome of someone who should never reproduce. And she has a tattoo of a butterfly on the back of her neck, you add.

So, is she your girlfriend?

You take the paper from L and crumple it up and toss it onto the highway. The wind carries it along the yellow painted lines, back to the town from where it came.

Did you go on a date, at least? L asks.

I took her and her kids to dinner.

Was it magical?

It was depressing.

That sounds magical to me. Please tell me that you fucked her, at least.

Could you do me a favour and not talk for the rest of the day?

L reaches for the cigarette hanging from your lips and then kicks over your suitcase and sits down, sinking into the empty space. Ow, she yells, struggling to get out of the hole. What the hell do you have in here? She unzips the top and flops it open.

You have clean clothes, she announces, holding up the plastic bag.

They aren't clean.

Why do you have a pail of chalk?

You take one last drag of the cigarette and toss it onto the highway. You try to close the suitcase, but L tells you to wait. She opens the pail and grabs several large sticks of chalk and walks away.

You're wasting time, you say, as L stops again and walks out into the middle of the lane on the highway. In tall letters she scrawls the words, Fuck you, in blue chalk. A kilometre down the road, she stops again and writes the words, You're going the wrong way. And again, she stops down the road beside the highway sign announcing the next town is only five kilometres away and writes, No one left alive.

Lie down, L says.

What?

Lie down on the road; let me draw your outline.

You keep walking, so she throws a stone at your back. Then do me, she says, already lying on the hot asphalt, the piece of chalk held in the air. You take it from L and outline her body in various poses along the highway. She bends her legs and arms to make it look like she is running, or curls into a ball in what looks like a prayer. With the town in sight, L lies down again and spreads her arms out. You tell her you're tired and hungry, and point to the town that is just ahead.

One more, she says.

Can we please just go?

One more, I promise.

You're being ridiculous.

Please.

Haven't you left enough of yourself out on the highway?

That wasn't me.

Then who was it?

I was pretending I was someone else. Now I'll be me for the last one. I promise.

You kneel down next to L and run the chalk over the rough asphalt, along her coat and jeans and over her heavy-knit hat. She keeps her eyes closed the entire time. When you are done she stands to examine your work. She doesn't say anything and you ask if she's okay.

I've just never seen my body before, she says, not like this.

It looks empty, doesn't it?

It is empty. Come on, let's go. I need a smoke.

In town, you walk into a restaurant and the cold air from the air conditioner makes your skin contract and tingle. You tell L to order you pancakes while you run across the street to rent a car. But it's five in the afternoon, she says. Across the street you request a car with air conditioning and you park it in the shade of the restaurant sign. When you sit back down, your pancakes are already there and you drown them in syrup.

Did you get any smokes? L asks.

They're in the car. You should go and wash your hands. L holds up her hands that are covered in pink, blue, and white dust. She rubs two fingers beneath each eye, leaving colourful lines over her faint freckles, and gets up from the table, leaving her spread of fixings for self-made fajitas. When she sits back down, the colourful lines are still on her face and you tell her that she's funny. She mixes the peppers, onions, steak, salsa, lettuce, and tomatoes on her plate and eats it like a salad, tearing off pieces of the flatbread and eating it plain. You order a hot fudge sundae for dessert and offer some to L, but she says she doesn't want any.

Can I bum a smoke? she asks.

Can't you wait?

Please.

You hand her the keys to the car and she slings her bag over her shoulder and leaves the booth. The silence is wonderful and you never want to leave the restaurant ever again. This booth will be your home in this town where no one is left alive according to the notices on the highway five kilometres out.

You pay the bill and sit sipping your water. Families come in for dinner and children shout and scream and colour on placemats with worn-down and broken crayons. You start to crave a cigarette, and you hope that L didn't steal your car with your cigarettes inside. You have the waitress box up the rest of L's fajitas and walk back out into the sun. Under the shade of the restaurant sign, you see a police car parked next to the blue rental that L is leaning against. An officer in a wide-brimmed hat is speaking to her, gesturing wildly with his finger in her face, his other hand on his hip, just above his gun, to push home whatever point he is trying to make to L. You approach and ask what's going on.

Is this your car? the officer asks.

Yes.

I caught this young man trying to steal it.

No, no, there must be a mistake.

He nearly backed into a family walking into the restaurant.

L looks down at her scuffed boots when you say again that there must be some sort of mistake.

Do you know this young man?

Yes and no.

Well, which is it?

Yes, I mean yes.

Look here, fella, the officer says to L. Look at me, I said. L looks up and he tells her that she's lucky this time. She scowls back and when she does, her cheeks perk up, and the officer leans in close to her face.

What is that? he asks.

Makeup, L says, rubbing her cheeks with her palms. The officer spins her around and sees the lines of chalk on her jacket and a strange little smile settles below his moustache.

Makeup, my ass. The handcuffs come out and L's hands are secured behind her back.

Get off me, she shouts.

You think it's funny, huh, writing curse words on the highway, body outlines?

L looks to you for help, so you say that it was only chalk and that it will wash away in the next rainfall. That's not the point, son. How many people do you think will see it on their way into my town? You nearly ask if he's crooked, but resist the urge, not wanting to get on the wrong side of the law again. L is placed in the back of the police car and you try to tell the officer that it isn't a big deal, but he tells you to step back and stop interfering.

She, I mean, he didn't do it, you say. You open the trunk and pull out the pail of chalk. It was my idea. We were walking to town after a bus accident. The heat must have gotten to me. I'm really sorry. I should try to set a better example. The officer looks at you and then back to L. He takes a long breath and opens the door to the squad car and releases L.

Come on then, the officer says to you.

What?

Get in, we're going to the station.

What?

You look out through the back window of the squad car at L sitting cross-legged on the trunk of the car, smoking a cigarette. You realize then that she still has the keys.

THE HOLDING CELL in this station is not as pretty as the one you found yourself in over a week ago. The paint on the walls is chipping, revealing the grey cement stone underneath, and the bars are painted an odd brown colour, like wood, and look like they could be broken with an axe.

You press your face back into the wood-coloured bars and try to remember how much money is in your bank account and if there is enough to rent another car. You imagine L driving the blue car with the windows down, smoking your cigarettes and listening to radio music. You imagine all the burns in the carpet, the scrapes on the paint, and the cracked or broken windows that you will end up paying for when the car is found abandoned in a parking lot somewhere on the other side of the country. Good for her, you think, and you envy her and the freedom she must be feeling, which has nothing to do with your face being squished between two jail cell bars.

You wake up several hours later to the sound of keys rattling against the bars. It is still light out and you ask what day it is. You are taken for fingerprinting and given the choice to pay a fine or do twenty hours of community service, cleaning up the highways to make up for your misdemeanour/vandalism charge. You agree to pay the five-hundred-dollar fine and before you leave you tell the officer that you think your car might actually have been stolen. No it hasn't, he says. It's right out front.

L hands you the keys and offers you a cigarette. You light it in the car and pull out of the police-station parking lot, while L licks her thumb and wipes the remaining chalk from her cheeks.

L KEEPS SCANNING through the radio stations but picks up only static. She says that she is looking for the weather report for the crop-dusting pilots, but you tell her to turn it off, and she does after one more spin around the dial. For several minutes you drive in silence down the highway.

I wasn't stealing the car, L says.

I don't care if you were. I don't care if you were going to steal my suitcase and my dirty shirt and pants and my pail of chalk or the car that is only a rental. It doesn't matter. I don't care.

I just want you to know that I wasn't going to steal it.

What difference does it make? You should have. You could be halfway across the country by now.

Did you want me to leave?

You don't say anything, so L goes silent. After several minutes of nails clicking between teeth, L tells you to stop the car so she can get out.

I'm not stopping the car.

Stop the car. I'll be fine.

I'm not stopping.

Just stop the fucking car.

Would you please just shut up?

Don't get upset with me.

I'm not upset. I told you, I just don't care. I don't care if another cow runs out in front of us and explodes on the windshield, or if a plane falls from the sky directly on top of us, or if I have an explosive aneurysm in my brain. It makes no difference.

Whatever.

L starts searching through her bag and finds the tube of Chap Stick. She lathers up her lips, smacks them, and pops the top back on. She offers it to you and it makes your lips sting. Instead of giving it back, you open the window and throw it out.

YOU PEE ON the side of the road in the red glow of the tail lights while L leans on the front of the car smoking and casting a long shadow in the headlights. There are still another twelve hundred kilometres to go before reaching home and you can't remember the last time you slept through an entire night. You join L at the front of the car and ask if she has a driver's licence. She doesn't answer, so you get into the car on the passenger side anyway and wait for her to finish smoking her cigarette. She is taking an unusually long time and you honk the horn, causing her to jump off the car. She flicks the butt at your closed window and it explodes like a silent firecracker. L gets in the driver side and turns on the radio, but picks up only static.

You aren't going to find any stations out here, you tell her, but she keeps going up and down the dial. Are you stupid? There's nothing on the radio. You slap her hand away and turn it off. I'm just going to try to get some sleep, okay? If there's an accident, don't bother waking me. Where are my pills?

What pills?

I had a bottle of pills. I think they are in my other pants.

You get out of the car and open the trunk and search through the pockets of your dirty pants in the plastic bag and find the little orange bottle. Back in the passenger seat, you shake out two pills as L watches.

What are they? she asks.

They're for flying.

We're in a car.

I realize that, but they relax you and help you sleep.

Give me some.

No.

Please.

No, you have to drive.

I'll take them after.

I don't trust you.

Suddenly you don't trust me?

I never trusted you to begin with.

L unbuckles her seat belt, turns to you, and says, you know, you don't have to be such an asshole all the time.

I'm the asshole?

Yeah, you're the asshole.

Just shut up and drive, please. I have to be back at work tomorrow.

Where do you work?

It doesn't matter.

Do you like your job?

You throw the bottle of pills against the windshield and pop two into your mouth. No one likes their job, you say. Everyone, everywhere, hates their job. You got it? Do you understand now?

L reaches for the bottle but you snatch it out of her hands. Take the entire bottle, she says.

What?

Do it.

Why would I . . .

Go ahead, you said it doesn't make a difference. So go ahead, take the whole fucking bottle, then I'll just kick you out of the car on the highway when you start convulsing.

You're funny. Now, would you please just drive the fucking car?

No.

Stop acting like a punk-ass kid and just drive the fucking car.

Why don't you?

I just took the pills!

You clench your fists and you can feel your whole body begin to shake when L starts laughing. You kick open the door of the car and start thumping your fists on the roof. Then you walk into the ditch and scream at the top of your lungs. The lights go out and you hear the jingle of keys fly over your head. What did you just do? you shout into the dark. You can see the outline of L standing on the seat and leaning out over the roof of the car. Now give me some pills, she says. You stumble out of the ditch, your head already becoming numb, and you throw the bottle at her but miss. You hear the little white pills spill out onto the highway and then see L bent over, a lighter burning in her hand, searching them out.

Why don't you take the entire bottle, huh? Do it, I dare you, I double dare you.

Okay, I will.

You run up to her, grab her heavy-knit hat from her head, and throw it into the dark.

What the hell, man? Go get it.

Fuck! you scream.

THE SKY IS so thick with stars that it's nauseating. You lie on the hood of the car, propped up by the windshield, and stare into the centre of the Milky Way. You can see L's feet hanging over the windshield from the roof, and she calls out another shooting star, but you don't see anything and suspect that she is lying.

What colour is your hair? you ask L.

Whatever colour I want it to be.

What colour was it before you had a choice?

Brown I guess, with some hints of blonde.

Why did you change it?

Because I wanted it to change.

There's another one, she says, but again, you see nothing. What colour is your hair?

The same colour it is now.

You've never changed it before?

No.

Why not?

Growing up I never had a desire to be anyone else. And now I don't think changing the colour of my hair would be enough to make me feel like I was someone else.

Is that what you think it's about, becoming someone else?

Isn't it? Isn't that why teenagers dye their hair, put rings in their noses, get tattoos of butterflies on their necks? To become someone, anyone other than the person they are?

I was a very timid teenager, L says. I never did any of those things. I went to class, I studied hard, I only sold drugs after school, I always kissed the boys on the cheek before I fucked them in the boys locker room, and my hair was the same colour the entire time.

I think you're lying.

You can believe whatever you want.

So what changed?

I did.

Did you want to be a boy?

There is a long silence and when L speaks her voice gets further away. I like people not knowing, she says.

Why?

Because then I can be anyone I want to be, at anytime. And if you can be anyone, you can also be no one, and it makes being invisible a lot easier.

If I close my eyes, you'll disappear.

L laughs and you hear the buttons on the cuff of her jacket scrape along the roof of the car. Do you think my body is still on the highway? she asks.

I doubt it. It's not in a basement.

What?

Nothing.

I went back to see it when I was waiting for you to get out of jail.

Is that where you were going when the police stopped you?

Yeah.

Why did you want to go back?

I just wanted to see if it was still there.

Was it?

Yeah. It just looked so empty.

There is a long silence and you watch a satellite that looks like a faint star float across the sky until it disappears.

I hope my body is gone, L says.

Which one?

All of them. Look, another falling star.

I don't see it. I think you're lying.

You hold your hand to the side of your face with your thumb in your ear and your pinky over your lips and call your girlfriend. You tell her that you are stuck on the side of the highway looking up at the stars and that you wish she was there with you. You ask her if everything is okay, if she is happy, and if she ever plans on having children. You tell her that you miss her and that you love her. You promise that you will do better and that you will change, that you will become any man she wants you to be. You will be a father if she'd like. Or a husband. You could be nothing, you could disappear, though you would prefer not to. Just tell me what it is, you say. I can change. It can't be that difficult. Can it? I could dye my hair. Would that be enough? There's no answer so you bring your hand down from your face. The headlights of an approaching car blind you with white light, and kids in the back of a pickup truck scream and shout at you as they drive past. You shake L's boot but she doesn't move. You roll over and push yourself up on the windshield, but your hand slips and you smash your face into the glass. You taste blood but manage to get to your knees. You see L lying on the roof of the car, her arms outstretched and hanging over the side. Her eyes are closed and her head hangs over the back window facing the other half of the sky. You see a spot of light streak through the sky and then another. You wipe the blood from your face and sit on the road behind the car and count the falling stars in L's half of the sky.

L remains on the roof of the car in the morning, not even moving when a transport truck blows past, honking its horn at the car that's halfway in the lane. You examine your reflection in the side mirror and notice two large bloodstains on the front of your lavender shirt, buried in the sweat stains and just above the spot where the gin made contact. You search through the grass for the car keys, again disturbing the grasshoppers that bound out of the way but do not click their wings. After searching for almost an hour, you find the keys hanging on a branch of a flowering tree with small orange berries that look sweet. You wait for the cars to go past, then search on the other side of the road. You pull L down off the roof and put her in the back seat, resting her head on her heavy-knit hat. You tune the radio to static and pull back onto the highway, leaving behind the stray pills and the little orange bottle, and start driving toward your half of the sky.

FROM A PAY PHONE outside a gas station, you call work and leave a message explaining that there has been a family emergency, which is why you were not in today, but you promise to be there tomorrow. You also mention something about a bus accident, but you realize after hanging up that that detail probably wasn't necessary. Then you call your girlfriend and tell her that you are still on the road. She isn't surprised that you didn't get on the plane, but she's worried about you missing work. You want to tell her that you don't even care anymore, but your job is the last bit of respect that she still has for you, so you reassure her that if you drive most of the night you will be back in time for work. You also tell her about the bus accident. She asks if you are okay and you tell her that you are. There is a long pause and then you ask her if she thinks you would look good in a lavender shirt. She tells you that she has to go and to call her when you get back to the city. You hang up the phone, hearing her say those last words again and again in your head, and you look over your shoulder to L and smile.

Do you need to call someone? you ask, offering her the receiver and a handful of change. L scrunches her nose and shakes her head, so you hang up the receiver. Let's get something to eat.

Dead animals hang from the walls of a small restaurant off the highway. You and L sit below the head of a black bear mid roar, its plastic tongue sticking out beyond its bottom teeth, making it look less formidable. Between the animals are licence plates from various states and provinces and old oil and pop cans nailed to the wall. L breathes on a spoon and hangs it on the end of her nose. She keeps it there while the waiter takes her order, and before he leaves, she asks him for another spoon. I'm starving, L says. You aren't feeling very hungry, so you order toast and a glass of beer.

I'm sorry, we aren't serving breakfast anymore, the waiter tells you.

Just throw two pieces of bread on the grill for three seconds on each side and serve it with a ball of butter.

The waiter, not feeling motivated enough to argue, walks away and throws open the kitchen doors. The spoon falls from L's nose and jumps around on the table.

Who did you call? L asks.

Work.

Did you quit your job?

No, I told them why I wasn't in today.

That sounds like quitting to me.

I didn't quit. I hope they understand.

Who did you call after that?

Why so many questions?

I'm just curious.

I called a friend.

An ex-friend?

Yes.

How is she?

She's fine.

The waiter returns with your toast and even brings two packets of jam and a tall glass of beer. A spread of fries, a steak, salad, and apple pie is laid out in front of L and she immediately cuts off a giant piece of steak and bites into it.

Did you call your family? L asks.

No.

How come?

I don't really have anything else to say to them.

It sounds like they are going through a pretty tough time.

They are.

Can you do anything to help them?

There is nothing anyone can do to help them. What Marie is going through is probably the most difficult thing anyone could ever go through. You see, there are people in the world who shouldn't have children, but do. But there are also people in the world that should have children, but don't. Marie would be a great mother.

Maybe she will someday, L says.

I don't know about that.

Do you have children?

No.

Do you want children?

I used to, once upon a time.

And now? What changed?

I just can't see it anymore.

Is it because you're broken-hearted?

I have to go to the bathroom.

In the bathroom you see your full reflection in an actual mirror for the first time since leaving the motel. Your lavender shirt is a disgrace. You sit in a stall and close the door, reading the names and phone numbers scrawled on the side walls. You wish that L really would get up and leave the table, walk outside, and steal the car. Then you could be stranded in this restaurant that isn't actually in any town. You would miss work on Tuesday, lose your job, dye your hair and disappear, and most importantly of all, you wouldn't have to answer anymore of L's goddamned questions. When you get back to the table, L is still there, the steak is gone, and she's working her way through the apple pie. You tell her that you need to stop and buy a new shirt. But you look so good in that colour, she says. You finish your beer and order another and L asks if you need her to drive.

I'm not an alcoholic, you say.

I never said you were.

I just want to be clear on that.

Okay, we're clear.

You eat the jam from the packets but leave the bread on the plate. You ask L if she has anyone waiting for her. She shrugs and slides your plate across the table and takes a bite out of your toast.

You don't have anyone? you ask.

What does it matter? I'm an adult.

Even adults need people sometimes. Do you at least have somewhere to stay?

God, what's with all the questions?

What?

I have to go to the bathroom.

You hand the waiter your credit card and he comes back two minutes later saying that it has been declined. You look in your wallet but find no cash, so you take the card back and tell him that there must be a technical problem and you need to call the bank to sort things out. But it's 7:00 PM, the waiter says. My bank is open late, you say, sliding out of the booth and weaving your way between the tables. You move toward the bathrooms and pick up the receiver to a pay phone nearby and search your pockets for change. The waiter watches you dial and you turn your back to him.

With the phone cradled between your ear and shoulder, you whisper at the women's room door for L to come out. You look over your shoulder and see that the waiter is gone, so you hang up the phone and open the door a crack and whisper for L. Who's that? A voice calls from inside. Who do you think? you say, stepping inside. You find L standing in front of the mirror with a tube of lipstick pressed to her upper lip and she asks what the hell you are doing.

Do you have any money? you ask.

Money?

I didn't think so.

You tell her you have to get out of here now, and start pulling her by the arm. Since when do you wear lipstick? you ask. You threw away my Chap Stick, remember? You both peek out of the women's room and see that the waiter is waiting on another table, his back to the hallway that leads to the bathrooms. You hurry out and he turns around just as you are about to clear the hallway. He calls to the bartender just to your right and you see a large man with a thick grey beard peer out over the bar at you and L. It is shocking to see the ease with which this man, with a large gut full of beer and fried food, vaults over the bar, so you pull L back down the hallway and through the swinging kitchen doors. You run past the prep line and the chef wearing a white beanie and out through the back door. You toss the keys to L and tell her that she better be a good driver. She peels out of the parking lot as the bartender and several members of the wait staff come running around the corner and into the parking lot.

Did anyone see? you ask.

Of course they saw, L screams.

Did anyone see the car?

I think so.

The licence plate?

Who cares? It's a rental.

What happened to all my money? you ask.

You spent it on gum and magazines at the gas station to get change for the phone. Why doesn't your credit card work?

I must have maxed it out on rental cars and vandalism fines.

Don't you have a bank account?

My account is empty until my next paycheque clears.

When is that?

Just keep driving. I don't think they are going to chase after us.

What if they call the cops?

I'm not going to jail again, you say, and tell L to get off the highway as soon as she can. She turns left down a gravel road and then she turns right, back in the direction of the highway. You're freaking me out, L yells, telling you to stop shaking.

How many pills did you save from the road? you ask.

I don't know. They are in my jacket pocket.

You dig through her pocket and find a handful of pills.

Do you really think you should be doing that?

I feel like I'm thirty thousand feet above the ground. I need to come back down to earth.

You force four pills down your throat without any water. L keeps driving, and after thirty minutes, you stop shaking. You light a smoke and tell L that you will have to share with her until you get back home. When she hands it back to you, you can taste her lipstick on the end of the cigarette and you think about how long it's been since you've had that taste in your mouth.

YOU SIT IN the middle of the road between two yellow lines. Fields of tall grass line the road on both sides and there are no houses, no power lines, and no telephone poles. You haven't seen a car since you stopped.

Don't you dare, you say to L, who places a hand in her jacket pocket.

I'm just . . .

Don't you dare.

We're lost anyway.

You lie back down on the road and stare up at the sky. Are there any planes? you ask. L looks up and says she can't see any.

Look, it's going to be dark soon. Why don't we just stay here and we'll figure things out in the morning.

I have to be at work in the morning.

I don't think that's going to happen.

You cover your face with your hands to muffle your screams. L tries telling you that maybe this will be the best thing that ever happened to you and you say that you are tired of people telling you that.

Telling you what?

Telling me that something awful could be the best thing that ever happened to me. It's all such bullshit. There's no silver lining. It's just something people say to make them feel like they've tried to help.

Well, you did say that everyone hates their job.

Of course they do. But we still need something to fill the time between waking up and going back to sleep again.

What about the money?

Yeah, I guess we need that, too. But people also use their job as some sort of identifier, or to gain some sense of pride. It's as though what you do from nine to five is the only thing important about you. And if I lose my job, then I really will have nothing.

I don't have a job, L says.

That doesn't surprise me.

Fuck you.

You hear a distant drone and search the purple sky. You see the white belly of a plane directly above you, still lit up by the sun that has already set at ground level. It looks like a toy or a model strung from a ceiling. It's just as surreal to watch a plane in flight as it is to be in one. A car's coming, L says. The drone gets louder as the sound from the engines catch up. Did you hear me? There's a car coming. The sound of tires on asphalt catches up, too, and you can feel the vibration in your body. Get off the road. L runs over to you and pulls at your arms, but you start swinging them, trying to fight her away.

Get away from me, you say.

There's a car coming.

She manages to pull you up, but you break free and fall back down, smacking your head on the road. L walks past you and you see her waving her arms in the air and the drone of tires grows softer until it comes to a stop.

No, no, you hear L say, we're fine. He's just feeling a little carsick and needed to lie down.

In the middle of the road? a voice asks.

I know, but he said it helped. Just go around, we'll be fine.

When the car drives past, you feel the heat from the engine on your face and you can hear the tires running over every single bump in the asphalt. Then the sound picks up as the wheels start spinning faster, and when it's gone, you listen for the sound of the jet engines from the plane that just passed overhead, but those are long gone too, chasing the plane and the setting sun.

So are you just going to lie there all night?

Yes.

Well, I'm going to go to sleep, so if a car comes it can just run you over.

Okay.

Do you want to die?

I don't care.

You're such a liar.

You don't say anything. There are clouds drifting in overhead and you hope that the stars will be bright enough to shine through.

I'm going to take the rest of the pills, L says.

Okay.

I will. I want to die, too.

Okay.

I'm serious.

I believe you.

You don't care?

I told you already.

You're such a liar. Why would someone who wants to die take pills on a plane to calm them down?

I'm not afraid of death, I'm just afraid of dying.

Whatever.

You prop yourself up on your elbows to look at L.

How would you like to be in a plane plummeting toward the ground? How would you feel? No one wants to experience that, that sense of helplessness.

All death is helpless, L says. You can't stop it if it's happening.

Unless you're the one killing yourself.

Do you feel helpless now?

No, I've never felt more in control.

But you won't be in control when a car tire slams into your skull.

If you would stop talking I could fall asleep and wouldn't even see it coming.

Fine, then I'm going to swallow this handful of pills, and as soon as they are down my throat, I will be just as helpless as you.

Okay.

Okay. See you soon.

YOU WAKE UP to the sound of a car honking and the heat from its engine as it passes. The sun reflecting off the paint nearly blinds you and when it clears your body, the driver leans out his window and asks if you have a death wish. L is lying next you, her head resting on your shoulder. You try to wake her, but she doesn't move. You tap her face, but still nothing. You turn her over and try to stick your finger down her throat to make her throw up. She gags and then bites down on your finger. Get your hand out of my mouth, she says, pushing you away. There are two indented lines on the back of your finger from where she bit down and you ask her how many pills she took.

I didn't take any, she says, crossing her legs under her body.

But I thought...

Yeah, well, I'm not that stupid.

Another car approaches and blares its horn, so you and L both stand and walk to the side of the road and wave to the driver as she gives you a dirty look on her way by. You light a cigarette and hand it to L. You both stare at the chalk outline of your bodies on the road and you thank L.

YOU DRIVE IN complete silence until you come across a sign directing you back to the highway. The tires click on the repair lines on the highway as you turn toward home. L climbs into the back seat and falls asleep. You feel hypnotized by the highway lines and wonder if you still have a job waiting for you when you get back. You think about Marie and your mother, sitting in that empty house alone, the two of them like shadows moving past one another, hiding from yesterday and unwilling to face tomorrow. You wonder what will happen to L. You think that maybe you should veer from the highway lines on the next bend and just keep driving straight. It wouldn't take much and it would all be over soon. It wouldn't be like falling thirty thousand feet out of the sky. L is asleep. She wouldn't even see it coming.

You pull into the parking lot of a bank in the next town to see if your paycheque cleared. You withdraw everything but eight dollars. L sits up and asks where you are. Nowhere, you say. She notices the money on the passenger seat and asks how much is there. Over one thousand, you say. Is it enough to get us home? Yes, more than enough. She climbs back into the passenger seat and counts the hundred-dollar bills. She has never held that much money before and she doesn't seem all that impressed by how small it feels in her hands. There are only another five hundred kilometres between you and your apartment, and if you drive most of the night, you will make it back in time to be at work on Wednesday. L turns on the radio, scans up and down the dial, and stops on a classic rock station and sings along to The Doors, Jimi Hendrix, and Iggy Pop. You pull back onto the highway and become lost in the sound of L's singing. You keep the highway lines to your left during every corner and bend in the road. You want to keep driving this way, even when you get back to the city. You will drive over the bridge and past your apartment and keep going, following every twist and turn the road can throw at you until you run out of gas.

If I had really taken all those pills, what would you have done? L asks.

I don't know.

Did you really want to die that night?

No. I don't know. I don't think so.

Why are you so sad?

You clear your throat and ask if there are any cigarettes left. You just bought a pack, she says, so we don't have to share. She lights one and hands it to you and you crack open the window.

I just don't know who I am anymore, you say. And neither does anyone else. Indifference can be a really scary thing, especially when it comes from other people.

It doesn't seem like such a bad thing, L says.

You want to be invisible now, but it's a different story when it actually happens.

Maybe it already is happening. You don't know everything about me. Maybe I'm invisible because I can't even see myself.

You ride along in silence until L asks, do you feel invisible?

Not right now. But I get the feeling that I will again when I stop the car and you get out.

L SLEEPS WITH her head against the window while the lights of the city appear. You cross the bridge and drive down familiar streets, but you feel just as far away as when you got on the bus in your hometown. You wish that L was awake so you could ask her what it feels like to not feel at home anywhere. You suspect that she has travelled a lot and hasn't called any one place home for a long time. You try to remember if you have any extra blankets in your apartment for L so she can sleep on your couch, because you can't bring yourself to drop her off at a bus station or a shelter. A fire truck drives past, its sirens and horn blaring. L sits up and looks out through the window at the city lights and says that they look like stars. You ask her if she needs a place to stay tonight and she tells you that you can take her home and starts directing you where to turn.

You drive back across the bridge and into suburbia. Houses lie hidden far from the street and the odd light shines through the trees lining front yards. You pull into a driveway at L's instruction and come up to a little house with blue window shutters and a red door. Do you live here? you ask. L nods and looks out the window at the house. She tells you to turn off the car.

When's the last time you were here? you ask.

I'm not sure; it's been a while.

Why did you leave?

I just needed something different. I always felt like I was missing something, so one day I went out searching for it.

Did you find it?

No. I realized that there wasn't anything to find.

So why come back now?

It just felt like the right time.

You both stare out the windshield at the house and see a light come on upstairs. I'm sure that your family will be very happy to see you. L purses her lips and tries to smile.

Thank you, she says.

I didn't do anything.

She reaches out her arms and wraps them around your neck. Then she takes a cigarette from your pack and tucks it behind her ear beneath her heavy-knit hat. She digs around in her pockets, gives you a handful of pills, and tells you to only use them in flight. You promise her that you will. You offer L the rest of the money that you withdrew from your bank account, but she refuses. You will probably need it more than I will. You might not have a job anymore, remember? The red door opens and a woman in a pink bathrobe steps out onto the front steps, twisting this way and that, trying to get a better view of the blue car parked in her driveway. L opens the car door and before she steps out she tells you not to go disappearing on her. As she walks up the steps to the front door, she turns, and points two fingers to her eyes and then back to you, mouthing the words, I see you. The woman braces herself against the door frame and then grabs hold of her daughter. You start the car, the headlights shining on them like spotlights, and you put the car into reverse and leave, the light rolling back and away until they both disappear.

You cry in the car all the way back to your apartment. You have to park two blocks away because there is never any parking on your street, which is why you don't own a car. You walk down the empty sidewalk under the streetlights, dragging your suitcase behind, and you pause in front of your building. You sit on the curb and light a cigarette, but only smoke half because you are used to sharing it with someone else. You take a piece of chalk from the pail, and you write a giant L in the middle of the sidewalk. It will stay there for weeks and slowly fade from the countless feet stepping on it, carrying it away down the sidewalk and past the spot where you first saw those strange, colourful flowers. You start to cry again and feel pathetic. You walk inside your apartment and leave the suitcase by the door. In the bathroom, you notice that you are still wearing the lavender shirt stained with blood, gin, and sweat, and you contemplate wearing it to work the next day. You decide that you will see how you feel in the morning. You walk past the answering machine with its blinking red light and get a beer from the fridge. You turn on the TV and sit on the couch as though you never even left. The room is dark, with light only from the TV, and it feels oddly strange and unfamiliar. When you look away from the TV, you catch the blinking red light flashing against the wall. You take off your lavender shirt and leave it on the couch, finish your beer, walk up to the answering machine and press the erase button.

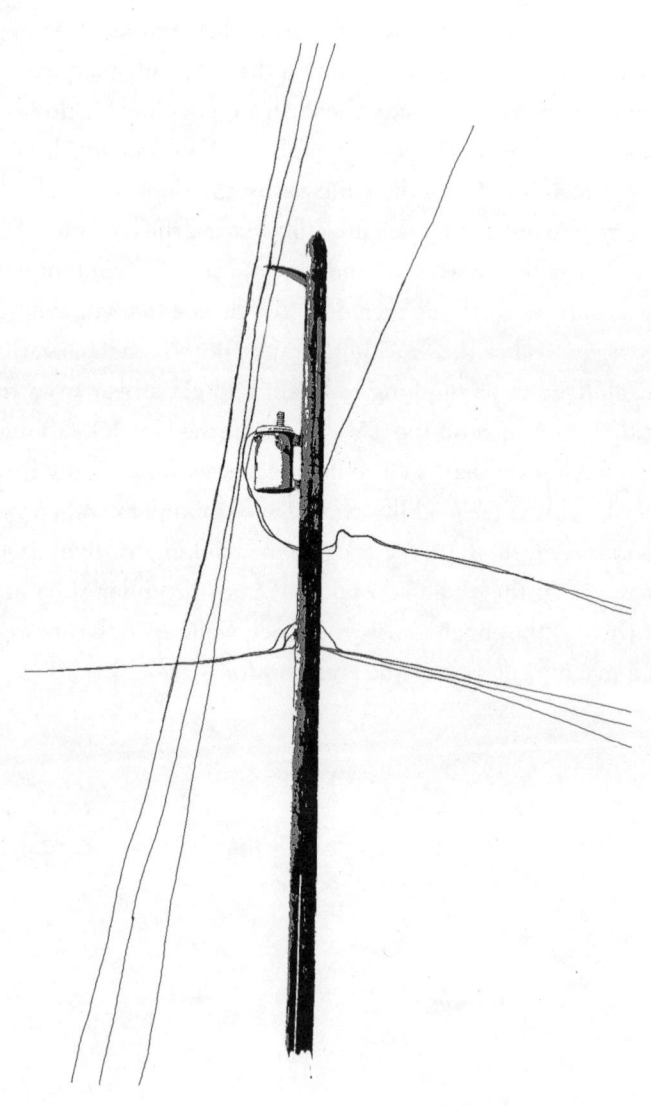

IV

Chalk People

The best thing that ever could have happened to you didn't happen. So you hold on to the last respectable thing about you and get up every morning and go to work half asleep and you can feel yourself starting to sink down. You work late because you prefer to be in the office when no one else is around. You spend most of your time during the day playing solitaire on the computer and hiding in the bathroom, and catch up on work in the evening. At home, you sit on the couch with the TV on but you don't pay attention to the infomercials or late-night news broadcasts. You twist and turn on the couch, your legs in the air, your head on the floor, trying anything to get comfortable, but nothing works. By morning you're not even sure if you've slept and you seem to pick up right where you left off, with the TV still on and still wearing the clothes from the day before. Then you get up and get dressed and start the day all over again. It's the same thing, day in, day out, day in.

On the bus, you pass by the brick buildings covered in colourful spray-painted lines, drawings of half-naked women, and the words *fuck* and *bitch* artistically scrawled in beautiful, inflated script. A child sitting next to his mother asks her what the word *fuck* means and she ignores his question. It means sex, you say. Fuck means sex. The child's mother asks what's wrong with you and you consider the question for a moment but don't have an answer. She gets off at the next stop and you turn to the woman next to you and say that some people shouldn't have children.

At work a co-worker hands you a card with a cartoon of a man balancing several files in his arms. On the inside, the cartoon man stands, head hanging low, looking at the files at his feet, with the words, Let someone else clean it up, written above. There are signed messages from everyone in the office, wishing the best of luck to a senior manager who is retiring at the end of the month. You hold up the card and ask the woman, resting her chin on top of your cubicle and having a conversation with someone on the other side, what she wants you to do with it.

Sign it, she says. Write something cute and funny.

Cute and funny?

Yeah, something fun.

You sign your name and write under it, You are retiring, close the card, and hand it back to the woman. She opens the card and reads your message and twists the corner of her mouth into a grimace.

There's a party next week, she tells you. Everyone in the office is asked to be there.

Asked to be there?

Yes, you should come. It will be fun.

As fun as the card?

What's wrong with you?

She stuffs the card back into the envelope and walks away. You stand and hang over the cubicle wall and ask your neighbour what he wrote in the card. He tells you that he doesn't remember and you ask if he will be going to the party next week. Yeah, I was asked to be there. He does not ask if you will be there.

At lunch, you sit on a park bench and eat a ham sandwich. You pull off the crusts and toss them on the ground for the birds. You loosen your tie and take another bite and throw the rest of the sandwich on the ground. You light a cigarette and the smoke drifts past you to a bench where a woman is sitting. She gives you a dirty look and you feel embarrassed, so you stand up and walk away, loosening your tie even more. You walk past a group of high school students in uniform walking down the sidewalk. A young girl stops and asks you for a smoke and you give her one. She tells you that she likes your tie and you ask her if on some days, she wishes she were a boy. You can see the tears start to form in her eyes as she walks away and it was not the reaction you were expecting. Before walking up the stairs to your office, you undo your tie completely and throw it in the garbage before entering the building.

Before returning to your cubicle, you wash your hands for fifteen minutes to try to hide the smell of cigarettes. You do nothing for the rest of the day and stay after everyone else leaves. The cleaning staff make their rounds through the office, negotiating the cubicles with vacuums, emptying garbage cans, and spraying nostril-stinging chemicals on mirrors and floors. When they leave they turn off the lights, not knowing that someone is still there, and you sit in the dark for another hour, your computer sleeping, and you pushing and pulling out thumb tacks from your cubical wall.

You sink further down. At home, you wake up in the bathtub, your head pounding, and you wonder what your girlfriend would think if only she could see you now. You dial her number, not realizing the time, and she picks up, half asleep and angry.

What is it? she asks.

I woke up in the bathtub.

I can't do this anymore.

You apologize for calling so late but she says that *that's* not the problem. You apologize for being the problem and, before she tells you she has to go, you hang up the phone and throw it across the room, taking the answering machine with it. The red light on the machine has not blinked since you pressed the erase button over a month ago.

In a bar on a Friday night, you sit on a stool and swivel around and around. You ask the bartender if there are any women dancing on tables tonight and he tells you to take your business elsewhere. You try to explain that you meant no offence by it and you order another drink. A young man with curly blonde hair is talking on the pay phone when you walk past on your way to the bathroom. You stand at the urinal, a little disappointed that there are no encouraging words scrawled in ink on the white tile walls. Two men enter the bathroom and walk into a stall together and you think that L would be pleased that they at least waited until getting behind the privacy of the stall walls. You knock on the door and tell them that your friend would be proud of them. You are told to fuck off, so you do.

All the houses in the city are lit up, every light in every room burning. You hate the person you've become. But it's no one's fault. You've probably always been this way. The people in your life just led you to believe that you were capable of being a better person. You keep walking into the night under the streetlights. A group of kids huddle together on a basketball court of a schoolyard on the corner. You stop at the chain-link fence and listen to them argue about some girl and whether or not she is as slutty as one of the boys says. You notice that the girl in question is among them and she laughs and giggles at the insinuations and you feel embarrassed for her. You're all punks, you yell through the fence. And your slutty friend will grow up to be a single mother working as a cashier with a stretched butterfly tattoo on the back of her neck and hating her life and her kids even more. They stand in silence, dumbstruck by a voice calling out to them from the street. You call them cowards and then they all start moving toward you as a black mass in the dark and you take off running down the street, hoping that the chain-link fence will hold them back long enough to give you a chance to get away. You feel like you could run forever and you keep pumping your legs, feeling like you are going faster and faster. You turn a corner down a dark alleyway, but decide it's too dark, and turn around. When you reach the street again, you run into the group of kids and tumble over onto the sidewalk. They swarm around you and call you a piece of shit, and a worthless drunk. You see the girl standing amongst them and you ask her if she's as slutty as her friends claim. Fuck you, she yells, and spits on you. The others start to kick you in the ribs and arms and then scatter when a car comes around the corner. Maybe it's your girlfriend, you think. If only she could see you now.

No one at work asks you what happened to your eye, which is bruised and swollen from kicks courtesy of teenagers who don't have any respect for women, elders, or drunks. In the bathroom, you bang your eye against the corner of the bathroom stall to make the bruise more pronounced. Someone in the stall next to you tells you to take it easy. Your eye nearly swells shut by the end of the day and people avoid eye contact with you in the break room. Or at least you assume they do. You can't see clearly anymore, and you never really noticed if they looked you in the eye to begin with. On the bus ride home you poke at your swollen eye with your finger. A young woman gets on at the next stop and sits across from you. You tell her you were jumped by a rabid gang of teenagers who appeared in the night and stomped on your face with heavy Doc Martens boots. The woman places earbuds into her ears and stares at her reflection in the window.

I admire you, you tell her, but she doesn't turn to look at you. You seem like a really good person. Your eyes are very pretty. Is that your natural hair colour? What are you listening to? Do you want to know how I hurt my eye? Did I ever tell you I was in a bus accident?

A man approaches from behind and places a hand on your shoulder. Sorry, mate, I don't think she's interested.

Oh, I wasn't looking for sex, I was just looking for a friend.

The bus comes to a stop and as the man pulls you up by the shoulder you ask if he wants to be your friend, but he doesn't say anything, and leads you off the bus. You stand on the side of the road and yell at the departing bus that this isn't your stop. You walk the rest of the way home in the dark, still feeling your swollen eye, and keeping your good eye on the lookout for any more roaming gangs of teenagers and a single slutty girl.

THE PHONE RINGS but you think it's the TV, so you search the floor by the couch for the remote and turn it off, but the ringing continues. You stumble over the coffee table and answer the phone. It's your mother. She tells you she finished her puzzle. It turned out to be a lighthouse. She says Marie is in the hospital but will be released in two days, and she asks if you and your girlfriend want to come down to see her. You tell her that you can't miss any more work. There is a long pause and then she tells you again that she finished her puzzle and that it was a lighthouse. She thanks you for helping her finish it and says that she couldn't have done it without you.

What happened to Marie? you ask.

She had an accident.

What kind of accident?

An accident. Just an accident.

But she'll be okay?

Yes.

You tell your mother you have to go. She tells you she will send you a picture of the lighthouse and asks when you will return the cup you took when you left.

You call your girlfriend to tell her about Marie, but there is no answer. You leave a message and tell her about the accident. You break down over the phone and for five minutes there is nothing being recorded except your muffled sobs and deep breaths. You apologize for your behaviour and hang up without saying anything else. You walk out of your apartment in your bare feet and wearing only a pair of jogging pants. You stand in the middle of the street and scream at the top of your lungs. You wait for a moment and nothing happens. You scream again and then wait. The city sleeps. You are quite possibly the only person in the entire city standing in the middle of an empty street in bare feet screaming at the stars. You admire your own place in the world and you decide then and there that you are a person of the night.

You show up to the senior manager's retirement party wearing your lavender shirt and a white tie under your suit jacket. You linger over the food table, picking at chips and pita bread, trying the various sauces and dips. You order a double scotch at the bar and sip it through a little red straw. A woman in a tight black dress, whom you've never seen before, stands next to you, waiting on an order of two red wines. You wink at her with your eye that still holds the bruises from a night one week ago, and tell her that you can't control that eye anymore. She doesn't seem to notice, so you turn around and ask her what department she is from at the office.

I don't work here, she says, my husband does.

Right, right, he's the office favourite. Everyone loves him. He talks about you all the time.

She tells you that you have a stain on your shirt and you look down and see that the bloodstain on the front of your lavender shirt is poking out from under your tie. I must have forgotten to wash it, you say. She spins one of the little red straws between her fingers and you ask her if she's ever been the one slutty girl in a group of teenage boys. The glasses of wine are placed on the bar and she takes them without saying another word to you.

You stand in the corner sipping a vodka tonic through a little red straw. Everyone around you is talking, mingling, laughing with their fake laughs, and smiling with their fake smiles. You want to scream. You want to scream as though you were standing barefoot in the middle of an empty street. The senior manager gets up to the microphone and makes a speech about how the last forty years have been the best years of his life. Will he still think that when he is lying in bed and about to die? Would he do anything differently? He spent half his life behind a desk and he calls it the best years of his life. You don't realize how loudly you are laughing, but no one turns to shush you. After the speech, while others congratulate him and pat him on the back, saying what a great speech that was, you walk up to the senior manager and take his hand. He seems surprised by the gesture and you lean in close and tell him that he's wasted his life.

Who are you?

I'm you thirty-five years ago.

He looks down at your open jacket and tells you that you have spilled a drink on your shirt. It's gin, you say. A deaf man gave it to me.

You go back to your corner when the cake is brought out, the candles burning like flaming jet engines. Everyone gathers around and sings For He's a Jolly Good Fellow. You take off your shoes and socks and slide them under a table. No one notices you walking around the hall barefoot, even in the bathroom, where you stand next to your cubicle neighbour at the urinal. You ask him if he knows any words of wisdom and he clears his throat. Do you have a pen? you ask. He zips up his fly and turns away. As he washes his hands, you look over your shoulder and shout: what about, *You are always helpless in death*? That has a good ring to it, doesn't it? Your voice is drowned out by the blasting air of the hand dryer and the flush of a toilet.

There is a half-eaten piece of cake at an empty table. You hang your jacket on the back of a chair and sit down and take a bite. You wash it down with a glass of gin that you sip out of a red straw. After you finish the cake, you put your head on the blue tablecloth and close your eyes. If only everyone could see you now, you think. There is a tap on your shoulder and your supervisor pulls up a chair. He asks if you are okay, and you say that you've never felt better.

I think you should probably head home, he says.

You suck in your cheeks and nod. I'm just going to grab another drink, you say, gesturing toward the bar.

No, he says, taking the glass from you. I think you've had enough.

Okay.

In a chair in the lobby of the hotel, you're woken up by a valet. You see some of your co-workers standing outside the doors waiting for cabs to take them back to their suburban homes on quiet streets lined with houses with blue shutters and red doors.

Did someone call you a cab? the valet asks. You can't stay here.

Isn't this a hotel?

Are you a guest?

No.

Then you can't stay here.

You walk out through the sliding glass doors and stand amongst your co-workers. They are all laughing at a joke that you just missed but you join in the laughter anyway. No one turns around to look at you, even though you laugh much longer than anyone else. Several people break away and get into a cab. The woman in the tight black dress stands with her husband, whom you don't recognize either, and she holds onto his arm a little tighter and whispers something in his ear. You walk past them, down the sidewalk in your bare feet, looking up as you walk, past the lights of the hotel guests that L said looked like stars, and are disappointed that you do not see any real ones, only the blinking lights of a plane overhead.

You wake up in a jail cell with all the other punks and drunks of the night, lying curled up on the floor or sitting on the bunks with their heads hanging between their knees. You are a king among men. You press your face between the bars and ask about your shoes. *Who's that?* You hear a voice call. A face appears over the desk and then retreats. It's lavender shirt, a different voice responds. An officer appears and tells you that you arrived without any shoes.

Arrived? you ask.

That's right, about two hours ago.

How did I arrive?

You walked through the front doors.

I walked in?

Yeah, you said that you lost your shoes, then passed out in the waiting room. I think you had a little too much to drink tonight. Look at your shirt.

You slump back against the wall and wiggle your toes. You can't remember if you have another pair of shoes in your apartment.

On the bus ride home, a man stands at the back of the bus and starts raving about being a castaway. This is his island, he claims, and he's the only one left alive. You can smell him from where you sit near the front of the bus and he wears a tattered grey coat and a blue baseball cap. Your head is still pounding and the other passengers start shouting at the man to shut up. You stand and encourage him to continue. He stares at you, trying to make sense of the man in the suit with no shoes, who is telling him to tell us more about the island he finds himself on. It's as though he has seen another survivor for the first time in years and he can't decide if he welcomes the new addition or if you are something to fear. You are convinced that he truly believes that he is the last one left alive and that he hasn't seen another living soul in years. The bus comes to a stop and you are both asked to get off by the driver. You stand on the sidewalk with the castaway and ask him, where to next? He looks down at your bare feet and tells you that you can't come. You have never felt so rejected in your entire life.

AT WORK ON Monday you are told by your supervisor that you no longer work there.

Am I in the wrong building? you ask.

No, you don't work here anymore.

You start to laugh and heads begin appearing above the maze of cubicle walls, watching you bend over, holding your stomach to try to calm the laughter. Your supervisor leads you into the hall. He apologizes and says he wishes he could have given you another chance, but there is just no place for you here anymore. He hands you a pamphlet for a rehab centre in the city and encourages you to get your life together. The middle-aged woman from human resources who smells like vanilla steps out into the hall and hands you a box of your personal belongings from your desk. Inside are a plain white coffee mug that has never been washed and a collection of colourful thumbtacks rolling around in the bottom.

You sink a little further down. You receive an invitation for your girlfriend's wedding and you are found lying on the stairs in your building by a neighbour who steps over you, carrying two grocery bags, and he tells you to get out of the fucking way. In the drawer beside the bed, little white pills roll back and forth, mixing with the thumb tacks you put there last week. You envy people in comas, who are like the dead but still living. You try to work out in your head how many white pills it would take to put you in a coma for the next thirty years, just long enough for you to reach the age of retirement. You spend the next two days in bed, staring up at the ceiling, watching the night pass by the window, and hiding your eyes from the daylight. Your girlfriend used to tell you that she only wants you to be happy. You told her that you want her to be happy and that she shouldn't worry about you. If only she could see you now. If only you could see her now. If only you could reach out and touch a little bit of that happiness she must feel to remember what it is like. If only.

You lie down in the aisle of the bus again and someone steps on your hand. You can see the imprint of their shoe and you look up and see that you aren't wearing any. Someone steps on your arm, then your shin. A child walks right up your stomach and chest, his little feet striking the tip of your nose as he steps over your head. You ask the pair of legs next to your face if the bus has reached cruising altitude yet, and the toes in the purple pumps turn inward. If the bus starts to break apart mid-flight, could you please jam those ugly heals into my eyes and ensure that I'm dead before we hit the ground. You are forcefully removed from the bus and you don't recognize the street you are on. You walk down the sidewalk and you feel like you are moving in slow motion. Everything else is moving faster than you are, like the world is flying past you at two hundred miles per hour, and you are stuck in a tube six feet off the ground. You touch the paint of a mural depicting a naked woman atop a unicorn riding across a rainbow that is painted along the entire length of a cement wall. It's beautiful. You sit below the unicorn and people throw change at another man lying curled up in a ball at the other end of the rainbow.

You sing along to the song playing over the intercom in the department store as you walk through the cold, white aisles. You try on different pairs of shoes until you find a pair you like. You carry the box up to the checkout counter and the young woman opens the box and says that it's empty.

Oh, sorry, you say, hoisting your foot up onto the counter.

You can't wear the shoes out of the store.

Why not?

It's store policy. She looks in the box again and then on the floor. Where are your old shoes?

You take off the new shoes and put them in the box while explaining that you lost them in a fiery bus crash several weeks ago. You can tell by the way she rolls her eyes that she doesn't believe your story and you love it when you tell a story that is semi-true and people still don't believe you. You pay for the shoes and as soon as she hands you the box, you open it and put the shoes back on. You move from side to side, looking at the cashier, and she asks you what you are doing. Is that a tattoo on the back of your neck? you ask. She picks up the phone by the till and calls security, so you leave the box on the end of the counter and run for the door, admiring how great your new shoes feel while running.

This is killing you. Life is killing you. You pace over every square inch of your apartment, your body twitching, the TV on, water running in the shower. This is killing you. You lie down but can't stay still for more than a minute, and you roll off the couch and across the floor, praying for an aneurysm. You suck the last few drops out of a bottle of gin lying on the floor and then light a cigarette. The smoke alarm in the room goes off and you pop off the plastic top and try to cut a wire with a pair of pliers, but it sparks and you throw them across the room and they become imbedded in the wall. The fire alarm keeps ringing and you contemplate jumping out the window. There's banging on your door and you lick your fingers and pinch the end of your still smoking cigarette. You open the door and are told to evacuate the building by a fireman standing with a mask covering his face and an axe cradled in his arm. Outside you look up and see the flicker of flames and smoke escaping from an open window on the fourth floor. All the other tenants stand on the sidewalk, watching a fireman ascend an outstretched ladder to the window. An elderly man and woman are led out of the front entrance with masks over their mouths, and their soot-covered faces are illuminated by the bright lights of the ambulance.

The fire is put out and the building manager announces that no one will be let back inside until tomorrow. You walk away from the scene in your bare feet, having forgotten your new shoes, and you stop at a bar three blocks away. The bartender asks you where your shoes are and you tell him that your building just burnt down. He believes you and gives you a drink on the house. For a long time you stare at a stick figure etched on the backside of the door in the men's room. It is performing an obscene gesture, but you look past that and concentrate on its face: its almost perfectly round head, the two dots for eyes, and the absence of a mouth. The door swings open and he disappears for a moment and then comes back, the same expression, the same black eyes staring at you. You tell him that he is beautiful and the man at the urinal tells you to take your queer ways somewhere else. You touch the drawing's face when you leave, and stop at the phone. You call your girlfriend and the answering machine picks up, so you hang up. You call again and hang up, and again, and hang up, until she answers.

What do you want?

There was a fire, you say.

Are you okay?

Yes.

You're not hurt?

I don't think so.

Do you have anywhere to stay?

No.

There is a long pause and you think that she has hung up the phone. Where are you? You give her the name of the bar and the street and she tells you she will be there soon. You empty a full ashtray in your hands and rub the ashes over your white undershirt and across your face and wait on the sidewalk for your girlfriend to arrive.

You get in the car and your girlfriend asks what happened to your shoes. You tell her that you didn't have time to put them on when you were evacuated.

So you've been walking around barefoot?

Only tonight.

You stop on the front steps when your girlfriend unlocks the door. She tells you to come in and you hesitate, thinking that maybe you could just sleep in the car, but she is already somewhere inside the house and calling to you to shut the door. It's the first time that you've been in the house since you left more than a year and a half ago. The walls are a different colour and there are pictures hanging that you've never seen before. She makes you a cup of coffee and invites you to wash your face in the bathroom. You stand over the sink breathing in the scents of soap and perfume and you think that this is what heaven must smell like. Your girlfriend knocks on the door and hands you a blue button-down shirt to put on. You take off your cigarette-smudged undershirt in front of her and put on the new shirt and the socks she hands you next. In the living room you try to remember what colour the walls used to be, and whether or not you hammered in the nails that now hold the pictures, while your girlfriend sips her coffee and turns on the TV. You ask her if she has anything to drink.

You mean alcohol?

Yeah.

She sighs and says there might be a bottle of wine. It's been a pretty rough night, you say. Did I tell you about the bus accident?

She returns with two glasses of wine and you restrain yourself from drinking it all in one gulp. She asks about Marie and mentions a message from you that you don't remember leaving. So you tell her again about the accident and your mother's puzzle of the lighthouse, leaving out the uncontrollable sobs.

It's good that you went to see them, she says. I'm sure they really appreciated it.

I'm sure they did.

She hasn't touched her glass of wine and yours is half empty. You tell her that you received her wedding invitation and you congratulate her again. I haven't replied yet because I might be out of town. I'm very sorry, I'm sure you know how much I would love to be there. She says she understands if it would be too difficult for you. She invited you because she truly does want you to be there. You ask her if she is happy and she feigns a smile and says that she is happy. You congratulate her again and finish the rest of your wine. She stands to take your glass and then sits down next to you on the couch and places a hand on yours.

You know that I love you, right? And I really do want the best for you.

You smile to keep the tears welling in your eyes from falling. I know, you say. I love you, too. She wraps an arm around you and you hold her tight, but this time you don't say that you never want to let her go.

Her fiancé returns while you are watching a made-for-TV movie. He introduces himself to you and you shake his hand. He comments that you look good in that colour and you hold up your arms, the sleeves hanging over your hands, and say that you might just have to keep it. You ask if he will be staying up to join you for another glass of wine, but he says that he has an early start in the morning.

I heard about the fire, he says. I hope everything is okay.

It wasn't my apartment, it was a room above me.

Well, smoke can travel pretty easily through those old buildings. But as long as it wasn't a big fire, there shouldn't be much smoke damage.

I have nothing to be damaged.

Well, I'm sure everything will be okay.

He shakes your hand again and you congratulate him on the engagement. He thanks you and tries to pull away but you hold onto his hand.

It's a lovely home you have.

Thank you.

I love the colour of the walls.

It's pearl white.

He tries to pull away again but you keep shaking his hand. Did I tell you about the bus accident?

THE FIANCÉ IS roused awake by your girlfriend, who tells him that the movie is over. He takes the two empty wine glasses and a full one and tells you that it was nice meeting you. You say that you will return his shirt as soon as you can, but he says there is no rush. Your girlfriend comes back and hands you a blanket and pillow. She hugs you again and you feel blessed. She turns off the light and stands in the light of the hallway. Before she leaves, you tell her that of all the people you have ever known, she will be the best mother in the world. Thank you, she says, and walks into the light of the hallway and flicks the switch.

You sleep on the same couch you slept on when things were falling apart. You cover yourself with the same blanket and you look up at the same ceiling and out the same windows and hear the same cars driving past down the road. You step out the front door and sit on the same steps and smoke a cigarette, occasionally looking over your shoulder to see if your girlfriend is coming, not wanting her to know that you've started smoking again. You're tempted to lie down in the street, to scream at the top of your lungs at the city lights, but you think better of it. There's no sense in ruining a perfect evening by being yourself. You go back inside, lie on the couch, and for the first time in months, you sleep soundly.

Where are you going? your girlfriend asks.

Excuse me? you say, as you tie the thin laces of a pair of her fiancé's dress shoes.

You said that you might be going out of town.

Oh, yes, I was thinking about driving to the ocean.

That sounds like fun. Which one?

It doesn't matter.

Will you go alone?

I might try to find an old friend to come with me.

That would be really good for you. I think you should do it.

I just might.

Can you get time off work?

It shouldn't be a problem.

She stops her car in front of your building and says that everything looks to be okay. You thank her for everything and you wish her luck. Thank you, she says. Enjoy your trip to the ocean. I will. You stand on the sidewalk, in your blue button-down shirt with sleeves that reach past your fingertips and finely polished shoes two sizes too big, and watch her drive away.

THE LIGHTS OF suburbia were always like a distant memory for you. You watched them twinkle across the river from the city, but the only way you knew what went on there was from television shows and late-night infomercials. You used to think that these neighbourhoods were the most depressing places in the world, but now you see them as beacons of a quiet life where people go to live out their lives hidden from the rest of the world. It is a kingdom of the forgotten and you feel like you are home. You drive the rented car up and down the twisting and curving roads with high curbs. You marvel at the giant brick houses that stand on hills like monuments to indifference. Sometimes you stop and look into the windows of the people watching television or standing around kitchen islands, talking, laughing, as though nothing outside those giant bay windows even exists. Sprinklers click and wash the driveways with water that runs to the gutters, and the distant drone of lawn mowers is heard no matter where you go. The sun is already falling behind the buildings of the city on the horizon by the time you find a familiar road and turn into the driveway of the house with blue shutters and a red door, which looks just as it did when you first saw it over eight months ago.

A woman answers the door wearing a blue apron the same colour as the shutters. She looks past you to your car in the driveway and asks what's wrong. You don't understand the question and you tell her that nothing's wrong.

Can I help you, then?

I'm looking for L.

L?

Yes, is she home?

The woman steps out from behind the red door and looks over your shoulder again at the silver rental car in the driveway. A lawn mower across the street hits something solid and it sounds like a gunshot.

Is she with you? the woman asks.

Who? you ask, looking back at the car as though there is someone sitting in the passenger seat that you never noticed.

Lisa.

You sit across from the woman at the kitchen table and she twists a dishcloth around her hands. It smells pleasant, like pancakes, and you look at the paintings of fruit baskets hanging on the wall, which match the actual basket of fruit in the centre of the kitchen table. How do you know Lisa? the woman asks you. You tell her about the bus accident and that you gave her a ride back to the city.

So that was you who brought her home?

You nod and she smiles at you, a gleam in her eye appearing beneath her glasses.

I'm afraid that Lisa is not here. We haven't seen her in almost two months.

Where did she go?

The woman laughs at your question and tells you that she asks that very question every time she disappears.

She does this often?

Oh yes, more often than I'd like to remember. When you brought her home it was the first time we'd seen her in almost two years.

Did she tell you she was leaving again?

No, she never does. She always disappears in the night. My husband and I don't even bother calling the police anymore because there is nothing they can do. She's an adult. We can't hold her down. But we always wish that she would stay a little longer, or at least tell us where she is so we know that she's safe. We really miss her. She was never really a handful when we brought her home. She did really well in school. But right before graduation she dropped out and disappeared for the first time. She only came back when she ran out of money and then she disappeared again. And it just goes on and on like that.

Are you her mother? you ask.

Foster mother. We adopted Lisa when she was eight.

What happened to her birth parents?

The woman spreads out the dishcloth on the table, smoothing out the creases with both hands until it is a perfect square in front of her. Her mother gave her up when she was only a year old. I don't know if she ever met her father.

Do you know why?

The woman purses her lips and says that she's already said too much and it's not really her business to speak of such things.

Please, you say, I would really like to know.

The truth of the matter is, I don't know the full story. I know her mother was very young when she had Lisa. She never seemed very interested in her daughter then. She was one of those mothers who never really appreciated the grandness of having a child. It was more like an accessory for her, a doll to dress up. Some people really shouldn't have children.

You laugh and tell her that that is the smartest thing you have heard anyone say in a long time, but she dismisses your laughter toward what she believes is a terrible thing to say.

I've met her mother a few times. She used to come visit when Lisa was still in high school and Lisa hated those days. She wanted to scream, I could just tell. Every moment that woman was near her, she would shrink down, like an abused dog. Now, to be clear, the woman never abused her daughter, not that I know of anyway, but it was just the presence of this woman that made her feel small, vulnerable maybe. I suppose it's difficult coming to terms with being abandoned.

The woman leads you into the living room to show you a photograph of L when she was still in school. She leans toward the camera to show off her goofy grin, and her hair is shorter than it was when you met her. You wonder if she believes—in the moment the flash of the camera caught the blood in the back of her eyes—that things will never be as good as they are now, or if in her vulnerability, she stumbled upon that truth long before, and that she smiles not for the camera, but because she already knows something others do not.

She was always a goof, the woman says. She always made us laugh. But there was something else, she just seemed so restless, like she had to do the opposite of everything I said. Just look at her. She always dressed like a boy, and it used to drive me crazy. I would tell her, you're so pretty Lisa, why do you want to look like a boy? She would tell me that she doesn't look like a boy and stomp away. Oh, to be in that head of hers.

You ask if she has ever asked L why she leaves.

Of course, I ask every time she comes back, and I get the same answer: I was bored. Bored. Can you imagine? Young people these days don't know how good they have it. You nod in agreement and hand the photograph back to her.

Where did you find her again?

On a bus.

And she was on her way home?

Yes, she asked me to bring her right to this house.

Thank you for taking care of her. It's good to know there are still good people left in the world.

You chuckle and shake your head.

You're blushing, she says.

An old habit.

The automatic sprinklers click on outside and the spray washes over the living room window. You watch the water hitting the glass for several seconds and then turn back to the woman and ask if you can see L's room. She leads you upstairs and opens the white door. The room is bare, with nothing on the walls, no books on the shelves, not even a clock next to the bed.

Did she take everything with her? you ask.

No, this is how it always is. She never keeps anything for very long. She sold all her books from school. Anything my husband and I buy for her goes missing within days. We used to think that she was selling everything to buy drugs, but, well, who can say?

Maybe she just likes to travel light.

The woman closes the door and walks back down the carpeted hallway. Then she pauses, takes off her glasses, and looks at you.

Why are you looking for her now? she asks.

I just wanted to make sure that she was all right. She seemed a little emotional on the trip to the city. I think she was just excited to get home and to see you again.

The woman smiles and touches your shoulder, then she hugs you. Her arms wrap around your waist and you hesitate at first, but then you hug her back, and you nearly whisper in her ear that you never want to let go.

Did she talk about home? the woman asks.

Yes. The entire time. All she talked about was getting home and seeing you again.

Well, that's nice to hear. That warms my heart.

Do you have any idea where she might have gone?

No, I can't say. But I'm sure she will show up again someday. She always does. We just have to stay here and wait for that day to come.

How do you do it?
Are you a father?
No.
Then you wouldn't understand.

A baby cries in a room down the hall. The woman excuses herself and walks into the room across from L's. You follow and find her lifting a baby from a crib. The walls are painted green and the baby is dressed in white. You cannot tell if it is a boy or a girl. The woman looks at you and says, like mother, like daughter.

She thanks you again for returning L safely back home and she offers to take your name and number so she can call you when L returns. You politely decline the offer and say that you might run into her again sometime in this life, hopefully not in the back of a bus. The woman shrugs her shoulders and tells you to watch out for the sprinklers on your way back to the car and then closes the large red door. You walk down the path, through the spray, and get in the car. You turn to the passenger seat where the pail of chalk sits, and say, as though L were sitting there, let's drive to the ocean. You back out of the driveway and wind your way through the suburban maze, looking for the road back to the bridge, back to the city, back to night where only you are invisible.

YOU SPEND YOUR nights driving around the city, parking in front of homeless shelters and soup kitchens, smoking cigarettes on the sidewalk and offering ones to the men and women who ask politely. You hang around men's rooms at bus stations and watch fifteen-minute segments of TV shows on the coin-fed sets attached to armrests. You leave messages for L in chalk on sidewalks and on buildings. You tell her to go home and that her mother misses her. You tell her that you're all right and that the best thing that ever could have happened to you has finally happened. You brush the dust from your hands on your pants and think that she's probably not even in the city anymore, and every time you think it your heart breaks a little. You never really knew what your intentions were and why you wanted to leave. It might have been the same reason that L gave her foster parents, maybe you're just bored. Or maybe, just like L, you're searching for something, something that doesn't even exist.

You try to imagine what you would look like as a woman and how it would feel not knowing who you are. Do you even know now? In a bar, you follow a woman into the bathroom and she screams and tells you to get the hell out.

Can you do me a favour? you ask.

I said get out of here, you creep.

Please.

She storms past you, smacking your arm with her handbag, and you can hear her shouting on the other side of the door. You look at yourself in the mirror, at your eyes, trying not to blink, and they look like they have been buried under ice for hundreds of years. Another woman enters and freezes by the door. She wears bright-red lipstick and her hair is tied back in a high ponytail. She sees that you are crying.

Is everything okay? she asks.

Can you help me?

She moves closer to you, like a wild animal approaching an outstretched hand.

With what? she asks. You point at the mirror and ask her to kiss the glass.

What?

Please.

Why?

I want to see what I would look like as a woman.

The woman catches your arm as you fall over. She helps you back up and you brace yourself against the counter. She takes out a tube of red lipstick and applies a fresh coat to her lips. She leans over the sink and presses her lips to the glass and holds them there for a long time, then pulls away. You take her place in front of the mirror, the red kiss she just left there now covering your lips. You look at yourself in the mirror, your giant red lips unsmiling, and your icy eyes above.

Well? she asks.

I can't see a difference.

You look very beautiful, she says, and then reaches for your face and starts to apply the lipstick to your actual lips. You can smell the vodka on her breath and she wears too much eye makeup. She finishes only the top lip when the first woman bursts through the door again, with a staff member following her. He pulls you away from the woman and she twists the tube of lipstick and places it back into her purse. She adjusts her hair in the mirror, the lips she left on the glass hovering just over her collarbone, and she turns her head to the side as though admiring the way her own lips look on her skin. She turns back to you and says, bye darling, and you thank her before being dragged out of the women's bathroom.

THE RENTAL CAR runs out of gas on the other side of the city. You get out, leave the keys on the front seat, and get your suitcase out of the trunk. You wander through the city, pulling your suitcase with the red piece of yarn tied to the handle, and the pail of chalk bouncing against the side of your leg. During the day you sleep on park benches or in hotel lobbies until you are asked to leave. It's surprising how much you can get away with when you are pulling a suitcase around with you. No one knows that you are not supposed to be somewhere. You are the living embodiment of transition, either coming or going, and no one cares enough to ask or wonder which one it is as you wheel past them on the street. You look at your reflection in the window of a restaurant. Your eyes are sinking further into your skull and you wonder if you're already buried under the ice. You order strawberries and take a bite of one and run the open berry over your reflection in the window. You are asked to leave, so you take a handful of berries and run out of the restaurant, dropping most of them on your way out, and stuff the rest into your mouth. You get on a bus and find a man wearing tattered clothes lying in the middle of the aisle on his side, his face hidden under his arm. Passengers step around and on him to find their seats and one kid puts his feet up on the man's hip and turns the page of his book.

What is wrong with you people? you scream. You see the eyes of the bus driver glance backward in the little mirror above the window, and the other passengers shift uncomfortably in their seats. Do you not see that man lying there? He's right there. There, right there, you gesture wildly with your pail of chalk. You place it on an empty seat and you roll the man over and try to pull him up. He opens his eyes, which are grey, almost lifeless, and he becomes startled. He starts to thrash around and his long fingernails scratch your cheek. You try to calm him, but he forms a fist and punches you in the face. Now you're lying in the aisle of the bus, too, blood mixing with dried strawberry juice on your lips. The bus comes to a stop and the driver marches to the back and throws you and the man in tattered clothes through the rear exit. You continue to fight and roll around on the sidewalk, the man screaming words you've never heard before, and you can't look away from those grey eyes. The rear engine of the bus roars to life and you yell for it to stop. The tattered man kicks you in the stomach and you whimper and keel over on the sidewalk. You nearly bump into a woman wearing running shoes who bounds over your collapsing body. The tattered man approaches again, but you fend him off by kicking your feet in the air. You catch him in the groin and he falls back against the wall and you scramble to your feet and take off after the bus. You run as fast as the growing pain in your stomach will allow until you have to stop and throw up on the sidewalk. The bus stops a block ahead, so you keep going, running in staggered strides after the bus, getting a little closer every time it stops. You finally catch up to it and jump in through the open rear doors. You search around frantically and find the pail of chalk on the seat where you left it. The driver gets up again and shouts that he told you to get the hell off the bus. You jump out through the open rear doors, cradling the pail of chalk in your arms, and take off running back down the street. You look at the clothes you are wearing: a green plaid shirt now stained with blood on the front and sidewalk dirt on the back, and an old pair of jeans with a tear in the left knee. They are the last clothes you own, aside from the oversized blue shirt hanging next to the lavender shirt in your closet. Everything else is in your suitcase, which is on the bus that has just turned a corner and disappeared.

YOU SAY HELLO to a man coming out of your apartment building, but he doesn't say hello back. There is no mail and you climb the stairs with your pail of chalk at your side and try your key in the lock. It doesn't work and you see an eviction notice on your front door. You sit in the hallway for several hours before someone notices you and calls the building manager. You haven't paid your rent in the last two months, he says. He smells of Aqua Velva and body odour and you have to take a step back from the halo of offensive smells.

I have the money, you say.

Well, where is it then?

It's in the bank.

Do you even have a job anymore?

I'm between things. I am just getting back from holidays. I took a road trip to the ocean.

He looks you up and down, at the bloodstains on your shirt and the tear in your jeans, and his eyes linger for a long time on the pail of chalk that you're holding.

Forget it, he says, I haven't seen you in weeks and I already have someone lined up to take on the place. Perhaps you can drive back to the ocean and find something on the beach with all that money you have.

Can I get my things?

He sighs and sorts through a large ring of keys and opens the door. You take a plastic bag from the kitchen and stuff your lavender and blue button-up shirt into it, but leave the shiny black shoes. You take what few pills are left from the nightstand drawer. There is no food in the cupboard and no drinks in the fridge. You say that the TV never worked properly anyway and everything else was here when you got there. You pass the phone and the red blinking light on the answering machine and leave the apartment. Several people poke their heads out from cracks in the door, watching you walk by, and you tell them that you won the lottery and are going to live by the ocean.

You sit on the front steps of your building until you are asked to leave by the building manager, who threatens to call the police. You step over the giant L you drew in chalk on the sidewalk, and when you look over your shoulder, you see the building manager scraping his foot over the pavement to wipe it away. You walk under the burning street lights and run your hand along the graffiti-tagged buildings and between the wires of chain-link fences. You step around homeless people sleeping on sewer grates and excuse yourself. You sleep on buses with the plastic bag as your pillow. You take two pills in the morning because you had a dream you were in a plane falling apart in the sky, and you pass out under a maple tree in a city park. You pick up the receivers of pay phones and dial phone numbers without adding any change. You tell your girlfriend that you no longer have an apartment and that you spent the other night sleeping in the middle of a basketball court at a public school. Then you tell her you're sorry for having called and for bothering her and you hang up the phone. You pick up the receiver when it rings and you are relieved to hear L's voice on the other end. Where are you? Why did you leave? Don't be silly, I can be there in twenty minutes to pick you up. I'll rent us a car and drive us to the ocean. You hang up the receiver and check the coin slot for any spare change, but it's empty, and you remember rumours that people would hide used needles in the coin slots of pay phones and you examine your finger for any puncture marks.

You quickly lose track of time and you measure the days by how often you are able to sneak into grocery stores around town and sample pieces of cheese on toothpicks or take bites out of apples in the produce aisles. You like to think that you are becoming an expert thief, but you get caught more often than you get away. You wake up in the drunk tank some nights, even on nights when you haven't been drinking, and your belongings are returned to you when you are released. The officer at the desk tells you he doesn't want to see you here again, and you frown, asking why he doesn't like your company. There's help out there, you know. You nod and tell him that you read a brochure once. You've been mugged twice, but you have nothing to steal. You fend off other muggings by swinging your pail of chalk at the heads of assailants and screaming like a madman. You sleep during the day and walk the empty streets by night. You walk down the middle of the street whenever you can, enjoying the space between you and the buildings that seem to hover over you, looking down at you with hundreds of yellow eyes, threatening to topple over and crush you.

You sit on the curb and suck on the apple seeds from the last apple you had picked from a tree in a suburban yard when you wandered too far away from the city. A man and a woman pass by holding hands and you tell them they are beautiful. The man turns and asks you what you said, and you tell him that he looks very happy.

Are you trying to be funny or something? he says. The woman tells him to calm down and opens her purse to look for money.

Save your money, dear, I don't need anything. Take him out to dinner but please don't break his heart.

The man pushes you back against the wall and you laugh.

Just leave him alone, the woman says. He's probably crazy and not worth it.

She's right. I'm really not.

The city is in constant motion, even at night. The people moving through the streets, and up and down elevators, are like blood coursing through the veins of a giant beast. Most move in steady directions, back and forth, to work and home again, to the mall and to Sunday dinner, and back home again. But you cut through diagonally, floating along on no particular path. You're like a virus, but one in which the city has never found immunity. It's not a problem really. You don't cause any trouble, aside from an unsightly rash every now and again. But this is where you belong, this is what you were meant to be. It's always been this way and you always knew it. Just like L always knew that she was different. She embraced it. Now you are, too. If only she could see you now. Why can't she see you now? Why can't anyone see you?

Today your girlfriend is getting married. Or at least you think this is the day. You can't be sure, but it must be today. It's today. So you cry loudly on the bus and ask every single passenger if they want to get married. Not to me, you clarify, just in general. No one gives you an answer, with the exception of an older man in a yellow zip-up jacket who slaps you across the face when you ask what must be his wife, and then slaps you again when you ask him. You find a discarded piece of birthday cake in a garbage can in a hotel and lick off the frosting to mark the occasion. You are asked to leave by the hotel staff and you ask for a plastic container for the rest of your cake, but it is taken away from you and thrown back in the garbage. You thank them for their hospitality when you are led out through the sliding glass doors, and when you step back out on the street, you run into your cubicle neighbour. She steps back after bumping into you, her head down, looking through her purse. You apologize, and she glances up, but you are already running down the sidewalk before she sees who you are.

You are halfway through a bottle of vodka you stole from a corner liquor store. The owner chased you down the street, but you hopped a fence and made your way along the train tracks. You slept on top of a boxcar until it started moving, then you climbed back down and jumped to the gravel below, your pail of chalk spilling out all over the ground. You gathered up all the pieces and walked alongside the moving train until it finally overtook you and rumbled away. A young kid sits down next to you on the steps of the building where you are drinking. He asks you for a smoke, but you shake your head. You offer him the bottle and he takes a sip.

You looking for something? he asks.
Like what?
You know, something a little stronger.
No thank you.
Come on, man, it will help take the edge off.
I have no edge. I am perfectly happy just the way I am.
Okay, that's cool. Do you live here?

You shake your head and take another long sip from the plastic bottle. You see out of the corner of your eye that he is looking down at your pail and the plastic bag between your legs.

You been on the streets long? he asks.

Who says I'm on the streets?

I just thought, I mean, you just kinda have the look.

You show your teeth in an exaggerated smile, thank him for noticing, and go back to your bottle.

I come and go, he says. My dad was a total asshole. He used to beat the shit out of me just because I was there and within reaching distance. My mother would scream and scream. He cuts the story off when he swings his arm around in a wide arc and strikes you in the face. You fall back on the steps, vodka spilling up your nose and in your eyes. You hear the rattle of your chalk being carried off by the young punk and you take off after him. Through stinging eyes you see him turn the corner with the pail in his hand, and your plastic bag in the other. He runs between honking cars and in and out of the glow of their tail lights, you following every step. He runs into a park and through a playground, not seeing the swing set, and flips over when he runs into the bucket seat. By the time you catch up, he is standing again, the pail tucked under his arm and the plastic bag wrapped around his hand, and in the other, a pocket knife with the blade out. He struggles to breath because the wind was knocked out of him when he flipped in the sand.

What, are you going to kill me for some dirty clothes and chalk?

What. Are. You. Talking. About?

You point to the pail and bag in his arm and he drops the bag and pulls the lid from the pail, his eyes becoming wet with tears upon discovering that the pail actually is full of colourful pieces of chalk.

Why the fuck are you carrying around a bucket full of chalk, you psycho? Fuck, he yells, and throws the pail to the sand. He holds his chest and bends over, trying to get the air back into his lungs, while you gather up the chalk again and pop the lid back into place. He is sitting on the edge of the playground and you dust the sand from the plastic bag and sit down next to him.

How long have you been out here? you ask.

I don't know. A couple months maybe.

How did you get here?

The kid spits dirt onto the grass and says he ended up here just like everyone else: drugs. I started in high school, smoking pot, then crack, and before you know it, he rolls up his sleeve to reveal the track lines running up his arms. How did you get here? he asks.

You laugh and tell him that you've always belonged here.

Shut up. No one belongs here.

I do.

Why?

Because it's where I ended up and I don't know if there was anything I could have done to prevent it.

Did you try?

I suppose not. But maybe I didn't want to. Maybe I just don't care.

The kid looks at you, his face twisted into a look so disapproving that you almost feel guilty.

Was it true? you ask.

What?

The story about your father.

Nah, man, I made that shit up. My father was just like everyone else's father. Same goes for my mom. They loved me as much as any other parent loves their child, but I just sort of faded away, you know. It was like, I was there, but I wasn't. Do you know what I mean?

You nod and tell him that you do. There are only a few mouthfuls left in the bottle that you carried with you throughout the chase and you offer it to him. He drinks it down and hands the bottle back to you and points out that you're bleeding.

I know.

It's on your shirt.

There's more from before, you say.

Sorry for hitting you.

It's okay.

That colour really suits you.

You walk with him back down the street, you in the middle, him on the sidewalk. Cars blast their horns at you and swerve out of the way and he tells you to get off the road. Where are you staying? you shout. He points up the street to an abandoned building and you follow him, still in the middle of the street, and once the street becomes empty, he joins you on the other side of the centre line. You walk up the stairs of the dark building, stepping over passed-out junkies and raving men thumping their fists on the hollow-sounding walls. Inside a large room, there are several people wrapped in old sleeping bags and a small fire burning in an old tomato sauce can in the centre of the floor. The kid slaps hands with a few of the others and sits down on an old sofa.

People offer you a seat, a hit from glass pipes, and drinks from unmarked wine bottles. It's a strange sensation being surrounded by people who know you are there and you start to feel claustrophobic, like you can't breathe. You are meant to be alone. Worse yet, you start to see yourself, who you really are, who you've really become, and you hate even more what you see. You turn to run for the stairwell, but stop when you hear someone call your name.

DID YOU GET my messages?

L passes you her lit cigarette and asks, what messages?

Around town.

No. I guess they didn't last very long, she says, pointing to your pail of chalk, its fading graphic almost gone and the white handle held together with electrical tape. You smell like booze.

It was courtesy of your friend upstairs.

Did he do that to you, too? she asks, pointing to your split lip.

We got off on the wrong foot.

Do you have any more?

Alcohol?

Yeah.

No, unless I can wring some out of my shirt.

Don't worry about it. I know where that shirt's been.

She takes the cigarette back from you and looks away. She still wears that heavy-knit hat over longer hair that has gone back to its original colour and the same green jacket, though her Doc Martens have been replaced by ratty-looking sneakers. She's lost weight and the dark circles under her eyes completely cover her faint freckles. Her lips are pale and cracked and you wonder if she still has Chap Stick, or maybe even lipstick, in the bag hanging from her shoulder. You ask her when she last ate and she just shrugs and starts walking down the sidewalk.

Do you still work that job you hate? she asks.

No, that ended a long time ago.

That sucks.

You're not going to tell me that it's the best thing that ever happened to me?

I wouldn't want you to think I was only trying to help.

You walk down the street in silence mostly. You try to ask her how she's been, where she's been, and where she's going, but she doesn't say much and just shrugs her shoulders. You tell her that you went back to the house with blue shudders and a red door to find her. L stops and drops the cigarette on the street and steps on it.

I didn't know you had a baby, you say.

I'm full of surprises, aren't I?

And you ran away?

If that's what you want to call it.

Why?

You're not going to lecture me, are you?

No.

You sit down on the steps of a building. The city is asleep. In the distance the lights from suburban neighbourhoods twinkle like ground level stars. You look at her staring at them and wonder if she is thinking of her. L opens the pail of chalk and starts colouring her shoes blue. Then she runs her fingers under her eyes and over her cheeks, covering the dark circles with blue chalk. She does this to you, too, mixing the chalk with the dried blood on your chin.

What are you doing here? she asks. What the fuck is this? Are you living on the streets now or something?

It's been a rough while, you say. I just sort of ended up here.

How?

I don't know. Maybe I was looking for something.

Did you find it?

Not yet.

Let me know when you do. I'd love to know what it is.

I will. I promise.

L lights another cigarette and blows smoke into the air. You ask her what her daughter's name is and when she saw her last, but she just shakes her head and looks away.

Why did you go back there? L asks. You tell her about the ocean, about trees that are so big you can walk inside them, and killer whales, and how you fell in love there. I think it was the happiest I've ever been, you say. I wanted to run away, to go back there, but I wanted to be seen doing it. I wanted you to see me.

Why? Do you feel invisible again?

You have no idea.

L closes her eyes and starts rocking back and forth on the cement steps. When she opens them again, there is a strange clarity in the way she looks down at the burning end of her cigarette. The intense calmness in her eyes unsettles you.

Have you ever hated someone so much that it's all you can think about?

The street goes quiet. You can hear the paper of the cigarette burn as L draws a long and deep breath. You breathe in the smoke from her lungs and smell the city in her hair.

Is it like loving someone?

I wouldn't know.

L takes the cigarette from between her lips and puts it out on the inside of her wrist. You slap her hand away, brush the glowing embers from her jacket, and ask what the hell is wrong with her. She brings her hands to her face and cries. It's the first time you have ever seen her cry and it breaks your heart more than anything else you ever thought possible. You can see the burn on her wrist and it's already starting to blister. You offer to take her to the hospital but she laughs and says that it's just a burn. She's had worse.

Come on, she says. Let's go.

Where?

To the ocean. She stands and pulls you up by the arm. She wants to go now, right now. There is no going backward, there is no stopping. She has to remain in constant motion. She starts walking away, asking what direction the ocean is in, but then stops and turns with her arms in the air, and sees you standing still on the sidewalk.

Go home, Lisa.

L closes her eyes and all expression leaves her face.

What did you call me? L says. How could you say that to me? Don't pretend to know me or know anything about me or what is best for me or for anyone else. Just look at yourself. You're pathetic. You run around the city feeling sorry for yourself, like the whole fucking world is against you. Guess what, the world doesn't give a shit. The world doesn't even know you exist. So stop blaming it for all your goddamn problems and stop trying to act like you care about mine.

You start to laugh because of how right she is, but this only angers her more. She steps forward and slaps you across the face and walks away.

Fuck you, she says, spinning around to give you the finger.

You run and catch up with her. No, L says, pushing you away. She tells you that she can't go back. She can never go back.

Maybe my daughter never knowing her mother would be the best thing that ever happened to her, L says. Did you ever think of that? Like you said, some people just shouldn't have children.

You want to believe that you were wrong or that she is lying. But who are you to say? She tries to move away but you pull her in close and wrap your arms around her. You can feel her face, wet with tears, press into your shoulder. You never want to let her go.

L steps back and wipes away the tears that have cut through the blue chalk on her cheeks.

I thought you didn't care? L says. Isn't that what you said to me over and over again, that you just don't care? Isn't that why you lay down in the middle of the road and told me to take a handful of pills, because you were completely indifferent to everything?

You think back to that night and remember the calmness you felt, how the indifference was like a blanket you had wrapped, twisted, and knotted around your body. But then you woke up and so did L.

It's true, you say. I didn't care. But not everyone is like me. Not everyone is quite so hollow. There are people out there that do care, that need you. They can't help it because they don't know anything else.

What about you? Don't you need me?

Don't worry about me.

L turns and starts to walk away again. The roar of a bus engine sounds in the distance and its white lights appear on the corner behind you. Through the windows you see that it is empty. You start after L, yelling to her that you know she wasn't willing to die in the middle of the road that night. L stops and turns.

Is that what you think? she says. I woke up in the middle of the road, just like you.

You stop and stare at one another through the darkness between the streetlights.

Did you know about her then? you ask. L wipes away more tears with her jacket sleeve. You didn't, did you? Otherwise you wouldn't have done it.

You don't know that, she yells. You don't know anything about me.

I'm glad you did, you say after a long pause. I'm really glad we woke up together.

L's narrow, cracked lips curl into a smile, barely noticeable, like it's not even there. She begins to talk, but you can't hear what she says because the bus passes you, silent at first, the flash of white in the corner of your eye, then the roar of the engine in the back like a jet about to take off. L turns and steps off the curb and disappears in the headlights of the bus.

YOU SIT IN the waiting area of the emergency room, tapping your fingers on the lid of the pail of chalk. There is a rip in your lavender shirt, stretching nearly the entire length of the left sleeve. There is a much larger bloodstain now, near the bottom, which you conceal by tucking it into your jeans. You rap your fingers on the plastic lid faster than before and look around the waiting room. No one looks particularly sick or hurt. Everyone sits quietly, some watching the TV bolted to the wall, while others stare at the floor. There's no electricity in the air. You were hoping for something a little more dramatic. You get tired of waiting. You've already made your decision. You approach the counter and say, I want to die. The nurse behind the desk does not look up, so you say it again.

I'm sorry, sir?

I want to die.

You'll have to speak up.

I said I want to die.

V

Chalk

The city is asleep. You walk down the streets and sidewalks unseen, like a hollow silhouette. You scrawl messages in chalk on brick walls and cement parking lots. You write the words, *No one left alive*, in the middle of empty streets, only for the words to be run over again and again by passing cars during the day until they disappear completely. You draw pictures of crumpled-up buses and cow parts on the side of a school, flaming airplanes on hotel walls, blue rental cars in empty parking spaces, and giant pill bottles on mailboxes. You outline silhouettes of yourself in various poses on sidewalks and laneways, highways, and one-way streets. Sometimes you give them little circle eyes, other times you leave them empty. You draw portraits of arctic mummies with wide, staring eyes in blue, and withdrawn lips in pink. You draw flowers you've never seen before on lampposts and telephone poles. Their petals blow across the street and up apartment-building fire escapes and come to rest on rooftops. You draw portraits of L, sometimes as a woman, sometimes as a man. You place bubbles above her head with arrows to her mouth, but you always leave them blank. You draw butterfly tattoos and hand gestures. You draw stuffed animal heads and pancakes. There are pictures of Marie and your mother, lighthouses, and frozen-dinner trays. You write out all the names you can think of in empty parking lots. Your father sits on a toilet smoking a cigarette and drinking beers from a tub on the wall of an apartment building, and around the corner, he dies in a hospital bed. You draw families and suburban houses with blue shutters and pink doors. You write that the past is yesterday and the future is uncertain, that death is helplessness, and indifference is a urine-soaked blanket we wrap ourselves in. On a wall overlooking your old office, you write, *the best forty years of my life*. You tell the city to be quiet, you tell the city to stop ignoring the helpless. You beg them to slow down, to not look away. You tell the people that you are already lost, but it doesn't have to be that way. You wish your girlfriend luck and remind her that she will be an amazing mother. You write your name, each letter a different colour. You outline yourself walking across the length of a wall, each movement a different silhouette. Your hands are perpetually covered in a thick layer of multi-coloured chalk, which also covers your face and your lavender shirt, which doesn't even look the colour of lavender anymore. On a completely bare wall, just painted red, you write the words, *Do you see me?*

The city sleeps and you pass through it completely awake. Your eyes are open all the time and you no longer dream. The pail of chalk bounces against your leg and the rattling sound inside grows quieter and quieter as you leave more and more chalk around the city. People brush up against it, leaving marks on men's suit jackets and scuffs on women's pumps. Cars kick up colourful dust that gets in people's eyes and in their hair. You ride on city buses and tell everyone that you love them. You sit next to people and ask them how their day is going, and tell them that your day is just wonderful. No one speaks, no one needs to speak. You let junkies and thieves beat you, clinging to your pail, waiting for their feet to return to the ground. Everything is dust, or chalk, the city completely dry. People look up at the clear sky, at the vapour trails criss-crossing the endless blue, and pray for rain. In men's rooms and women's rooms you kiss mirrors with lipstick-covered lips so people can see themselves as someone else. You continue to make phone calls without any change and you laugh and you cry and you tell the receiver that everything is going to be okay.

You see people that you recognize: co-workers, neighbours, the cashier from the grocery store with the ponytail on the side. You cross the street and follow her all the way to the grocery store. Outside the store, you draw her picture on the wall to tell her that she's beautiful. You see your girlfriend walking through the park holding hands with her husband and you smile. You walk through back alleys and outline the homeless with white chalk, so when they disappear into non-existent memory, they can still be seen. You write and you draw and you sketch until your hands crack and bleed, until you cough out plumes of chalk into the air, until your lips feel brittle and your eyes seal shut. You do it until all the chalk is nearly gone and you no longer have the strength to lift the tiny, brittle, worn pieces out of the pail.

You draw another portrait of L on the sidewalk and lie down next to it, curled up into a ball, and outline your body with the last piece. It breaks in your hand and is crushed under the feet of people passing by, carried away on the soles of people's shoes. You remain there, a little ball of chalk on the street, the portrait of L scuffed and smeared and blown down the sidewalk. You remain there until there is nothing left to hold onto, and then you run up the wall, your silhouette gliding over the bricks and across the street, changing shapes, and always staring up at the sky.

You pass under cars and cower under buses. You run over the bridge and into suburban neighbourhoods where you mix with rainbows and flowers left on playgrounds by school children. You move up driveways to houses with blue shutters and red doors and disappear on the white walls and listen to a baby's cries in a foster mother's arms. You twist up and down telephone poles and listen to your girlfriend singing to herself as she plants flowers in the front yard of her house. You fly across the country on highways, counting the yellow lines as you go, and you come to rest on red-painted fire hydrants and see Marie pushing a little girl on a swing at the park and your mother in the kitchen, her hand holding a puzzle piece, hovering over a picture of a covered bridge, and stacks of frozen-dinner trays soaking in the sink. You fly from your hometown, never leaving the pavement, and go all the way to the ocean, where you can only see the sky and the tops of trees and only hear the sound of the ocean washing over rocks. Back home, you move around the city, under people's feet, being stepped on and ignored, kicked and scuffed. You move through your own drawings, and touch the portraits of the people you left behind. You spin, twirl, twist, contort yourself around corners and under dumpsters. At night you stare up at the sky and look for falling stars, first in one half, and then the other. You wonder if people ever stop to look at you, to wonder who you are or who you were, what was inside this empty space.

You move around the city when it's asleep and when it's awake. You keep moving, always moving, always watching, always looking, always listening. And then one day, you stop. You look up and see an apartment building, not unlike your own. It is an old brick building, with four floors, and narrow windows. It's dark and there is only one light on. There are no stars tonight. You see the black silhouette of a man or a woman in the window and you wonder if he sees you on the sidewalk. Is she watching you? Is he thinking about you? You want to believe that he sees you, that he is looking down at you and thinking about how he's never seen this particular person ever before. And then you feel it, a drop of rain. Then another, and another, and another.

ACKNOWLEDGEMENTS

I would like to thank all of the organizers, judges, and volunteers at the 3-Day Novel Contest and the Geist Foundation. Congratulations to all the writers who participated in the 38th Annual 3-Day Novel Contest. You are all literary warriors and should be proud of what you have accomplished. Thank you to Brian, Karen, and Anastasia at Anvil Press for all their help, guidance, and making this possible. And a big thanks to Derek von Essen for a wonderful cover. Thank you to all the members of the Northwestern Ontario Writer's Workshop for all your support and encouragement.

A special thank you to Jodene Wylie for being the witness to my three-day ordeal, for always believing I could do it, even when I didn't, and for encouraging me to imagine, hope, take chances, persevere, laugh, and smile.

And finally, thank you to my family for all their love and support, who are proud of me no matter what I do, and for teaching me the value of reading, writing, and being myself.

ABOUT THE AUTHOR

Doug Diaczuk is a writer and journalist living in Thunder Bay. He has a master's degree in English Literature from Lakehead University. *Chalk* is his first published novel.